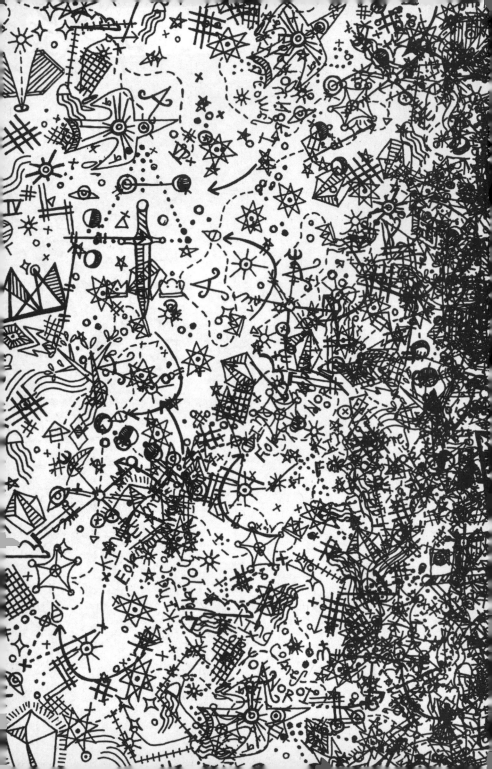

THE
WICKER
KING

K. ANCRUM

{Imprint}
MAKE YOUR MARK

New York

An imprint of Macmillan Publishing Group, LLC
175 Fifth Avenue
New York, NY 10010
fiercereads.com

Square Fish and the Square Fish logo are trademarks of Macmillan and
are used by Imprint under license from Macmillan.

Our books may be purchased in bulk for promotional, educational, or
business use. Please contact your local bookseller or the Macmillan
Corporate and Premium Sales Department at (800) 221-7945 ext. 5442
or by email at MacmillanSpecialMarkets@macmillan.com.

Library of Congress Cataloging-in-Publication Data is available.

ISBN 978-1-250-10155-6 (paperback) / ISBN 978-1-250-10156-3 (ebook)

[Imprint]
MAKE YOUR MARK

@ImprintReads
Originally published in the United States by Imprint
First Square Fish edition, 2018
Book designed by Ellen Duda
Square Fish logo designed by Filomena Tuosto
Imprint logo designed by Amanda Spielman

10 9 8 7 6 5 4 3 2 1

LEXILE: HL620L

On disposal:
If you skip recycling and toss in the trash,
something you love will burn to ash.

This book is dedicated to all the kids whose arms are filled with too much for them to hold, but who are trying their best not to drop a single thing.

I see you and I am proud of you for trying.

MINDEN CITY POLICE

BOOKING REPORT

							CASE NUMBER	DATE BOOKED
							2002-456769	01/30/2003
							CURRENT CELL	CUSTODY CLASSIFICATION
							5	1

SUBJECT NAME - LAST	SUBJECT NAME - FIRST	SUBJECT NAME - MI	IMAGE
Bateman	August		

RACE	SEX	DATE OF BIRTH	AGE	HEIGHT	WEIGHT	HAIR	EYE
mixed	M	6/21/1985	17	6'0"	167 lbs	black	brown

ADDRESS	PHONE
8329 Rocky Rd Minden, MI 49793	989-555-2030

SCARS - MARKS - TATTOOS	OCCUPATION
Tattoo on neck	Student

DATE OF INCIDENT	TIME OF INCIDENT	LOCATION OF INCIDENT	REPORTING OFFICER	ADDITIONAL IMAGE
01/30/2003	8:00 PM	Priorson & Co. factory	Timothy Smith	

CHARGES

1 - FIRST DEGREE ARSON / statute # 750.72

2 - TRESPASSING / statute # 750.552

3 -

4 -

5 -

6 -

7 -

JUVENILE INFO CODE	PA-PARENT	FP-GRANDPARENT	SP-STEPPARENT	GA- GUARDIAN	OFM- OTHER FAMILY MEMBER	THUMBPRINT
CODE PA	NAME (LAST, FIRST, MIDDLE) Bateman, Allison			ADDRESS 8329 Rocky Rd Minden, MI 49793		

PERSON NOTIFIED OF JUVENILE CUSTODY	RELATIONSHIP	HOW NOTIFIED	DATE/TIME NOTIFIED
Allison Bateman	mother	phone	01/30/03 9:30 PM

ADDRESS	PHONE

NOTES

Subject required medical attention prior to arrest. Subject taken into custody and transported to Minden City police department for interview and booking. Subject later transported to Minden Detention Facility for holding.

OFFICER SIGNATURE	BADGE	SUPERVISOR SIGNATURE	FULL PRINTS ON FILE
	21001		ASSIGNED TO

1998

They were thirteen the first time they broke into the toy factory.

It was almost midnight, it was freezing outside, and August was fucking terrified. He pushed his dark hair out of his face, plastering himself to Jack's back while Jack tried to jimmy the handle open.

"Come on, *come on*. You're so slow. We're going to get caught, you asshole," he whispered.

Jack ignored him. August always got mean when he was scared.

After a couple more seconds of watching Jack rattle the handle, August gave up on that approach entirely and just threw a brick through the window instead.

They both flinched at the sound of breaking glass and ducked farther into the shadows. When the police didn't burst out of nowhere and arrest them immediately, August turned back to Jack and grinned.

Jack punched him in the arm and grinned back. "Quit showing off. Race you inside?"

"Thank you, August, for getting us in. I don't know what I would do without you. Oh, you're welcome, Jack. Anything for you, princess," August deadpanned.

Jack pushed him. "Why are you such a dick? Just get inside."

They crawled in through the broken window and dropped down to the floor.

"Whoa."

"Did you bring your flashlight?"

"No, Jack. I followed you through the night to break into an abandoned building without a flashlight."

"Seriously. Stop bitching. What is wrong with you?"

"I'm *scared*. I feel like I'm trapped with you in a more terrifying version of *Bridge to Terabithia*."

"You're not. And you need to stop reading books like that. Now give me your flashlight."

August handed it over miserably.

Jack turned it on, the dim light bringing out the hollows of his face. "Oh yeah. Ha ha ha, *wow*. Yeah, this might be the best place in the whole town. We are *definitely* coming back here in the morning."

And even though Jack's word was pretty much law, August fervently prayed that they wouldn't go back ever again.

MINDEN CITY POLICE

ARREST REPORT

DIVISION ATTENDING: 743	DIVISION REPORTING: 743 DX NO:
DATE AND TIME OF ARREST: 01/30/2003	CHARGES: First degree arson, trespassing
LOCATION OF ARREST: Minden Forest Preserve	CHARGED AT: Minden City Police Department

PERSON ARRESTED: Bateman, August   ALIAS:

AGE: 17   SEX: M   OCCUPATION: Student

ADDRESS: 8329 Rocky Rd, Minden, MI 49793

PARENTS: MOTHER: Allison Bateman   FATHER:

ADDRESS: 8329 Rocky Rd   ADDRESS:
Minden, MI 49793

CASE NUMBER: 2002-456769

ARREST OFFICER: Timothy Smith   BADGE: 21001

REPORT:

Officer Suffern and I responded to a call from multiple Minden City residents about black smoke coming from the east entrance to the Minden Forest Preserve. The Fire Department had also been called and was present when we arrived at the scene. The Priorson and Co. factory was on fire. There was physical evidence that the fire had been set intentionally. A gasoline canister as well as several rags were on the scene.

Officer Suffern apprehended the suspects, two students from Barnard High School: August Bateman, 17, and Jack Rossi, 17.

Upon further inspection of the suspects I confirmed that suspect August Bateman was in severe need of medical attention that delayed his arrest by over an hour. Suspect was compliant with both on-site medical treatment and arrest.

Jack Rossi was apprehended as well, but seemed very disoriented and resisted arrest. Suspect also appears to have vision problems that contradict his involvement in the fire, but he insisted verbally that he be taken in and booked with August Bateman.

There was no damage to the surrounding Forest Preserve. Besides the Fire Department, emergency personnel, Officer Suffern and myself, there were no other witnesses.

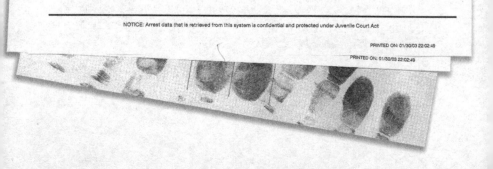

2003

It was August's third night in the asylum, and already he had learned several things:

1. It was never a comfortable temperature. Ever. It was always too warm or too cold.
2. Only roughly half of the rules made logical sense. The other half seemed deliberately designed to be broken accidentally.
3. You ate when they told you to and you ate what they told you to, or you didn't eat at all. (Then you got punished for that, too.)
4. No one had real blankets.
5. No one had real friends.
6. This was maybe worse than jail.

His roommate was terrified of him and wouldn't speak to him because they'd brought him into the hospital in handcuffs, straight from court, and the orderlies didn't have the kindness to explain to everyone that he wasn't actually a crazed serial murderer.

He wasn't allowed to have pencils or be unsupervised, because for some strange reason he was on suicide watch. They also made him wear a red uniform to separate him from the rest of the patients so it was clear he was a special prisoner-patient. As if the "handcuffed prison-guard parade" wasn't enough.

And worst of all—he had never wanted a cigarette more in his goddamn life.

But it would be a cold day in hell before that happened. They don't give lighters to arsonists.

AUGUST

He probably would have gotten off easier if he hadn't been so sarcastic.

It was just—they kept asking the *stupidest* questions. You know how small-town cops are. It was way too difficult to hold it in.

"Was the fire an accident, son?" The officer had looked tired, like he hoped August would say yes.

But, of course, August didn't. He'd just narrowed his eyes and said something rude. Then they slammed him into the holding cell so fast, it was as if he'd been begging to go.

Honestly, though. He was standing there with accelerant drying on his jeans and second-degree burns on his hands. It was a waste of everyone's time to try lying.

JACK

It was mostly his own fault for getting dragged in. But August supposed if he could blame anyone else for his current situation, it would be Jack.

Jack had always been bossy—even when they were kids. He didn't leave much room for defiance when his mind was set on something, and August had just gotten used to it. He wasn't a leader. It wasn't natural for him. He understood and accepted that. But . . . sometimes it's better to have control over your own destiny.

This situation was one of those times.

Which—August thought as he tested the restraints on his wrists—was a grievous understatement.

Besides, he felt kind of bad complaining so much. Jack was doing ten *thousand* times worse than he was. The poor kid couldn't even go outside.

But—like every disaster they'd gotten themselves into through the history of their friendship—it hadn't started all bad. Things were actually pretty fun until that last bit with all the screaming and the flames and the ambulances.

ROOSEVELT HIGH SCORE

They didn't hang out at school, Jack and him. They were on *stratospherically* different popularity levels. Plus, these types of things usually had a system:

The Jocks stuck to the Jocks, the Punk kids with the Punk kids, Band Geeks, Goths, AP hard-asses, agro ROTC-ers, Stoners, Ravers, Cheerleaders, New Age Hippies, Hipsters, Grunge Kids, Gamers, Lit Nerds, Actual Nerds, Theater Kids, Druggies, Gangsters, "the Popular Crowd," and those shy, immature kids who grouped together in awkward clumps. Everyone stuck to what they knew.

Of course, there was drifting between subgroups, but it was rare.

Jack rode the edge of the Popular Crowd just by virtue of his involvement with sports, while August found himself smack between the Lit Nerds and the Druggies—roughly near the middle of the totem. It wasn't exactly glamorous, but running drugs for Daliah meant that he was part of a group of Providers of Services—notable figureheads of the high school economy—and that he could make a month's worth of "minimum wage part-time job" wages in a week. Which was important because he really needed the money.

He didn't brag about it, but the way he looked really helped with not getting caught. August was horribly neat and organized.

He wore fashionable, expensive clothes that he saved up for months to buy, and he was intense about personal hygiene. He didn't like people to know that he was poor. So he was never on a suspect list because of his obvious fastidiousness, spotless record, and absolutely *perfect* slicked-back hair.

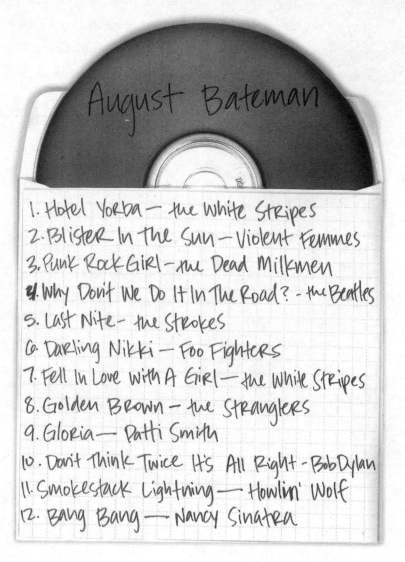

August Bateman

1. Hotel Yorba — the White Stripes
2. Blister In The Sun — Violent Femmes
3. Punk Rock Girl — the Dead Milkmen
4. Why Don't We Do It In The Road? - the Beatles
5. Last Nite — the Strokes
6. Darling Nikki — Foo Fighters
7. Fell In Love With A Girl — the White Stripes
8. Golden Brown — the Stranglers
9. Gloria — Patti Smith
10. Don't Think Twice It's All Right - Bob Dylan
11. Smokestack Lightning — Howlin' Wolf
12. Bang Bang — Nancy Sinatra

WOLVES

They really only saw each other on school property at games. Their rugby team wasn't the best, but since it was the only major sport in their town, everyone generally made a lot of hoopla about it.

August didn't even like rugby, but he went to every game anyway. Jack was ridiculously athletic and first line this year, so August couldn't make an excuse not to care. He never cheered, because that was too much work. But he went, and that seemed to be enough.

After games, they usually met up in the locker room before taking Jack's shitty Camaro out to the plains to fuck around in the grass.

Wrestle and run. That sort of thing.

It was tradition. It made it all right that they didn't see each other during the day. It was worth people not knowing that they knew each other better than anyone knew *anyone*, really. They were so far apart on the social spectrum that it wouldn't make sense to people if they started openly hanging out together. It would be a spectacle, and August didn't like spectacle. Some things were just meant to be private.

CARRIE-ANNE

Jack was good-looking. He was a bit shorter than August, but not by much. He had a sharp face with clever eyes, and usually wore his hair buzzed low—but it had grown out now. He had the whole *light hair–gray eyes* thing going on that people went crazy for. He was also strong and athletic. That didn't mean much to August, but he'd heard girls talking about it in the hallway.

Jack was popular, unlike August, and of course he had a girl-friend. Her name was Carrie-Anne: a bottle-blond, UGG-booted, North Face–wearing prepster with a perfect GPA.

August *loathed* her.

He could've written sonnets about her pouty lips and golden hair and ivory skin and melodious voice. Not because he admired those things in the slightest—he couldn't have cared less about the way she looked. It was because he had to constantly listen to Jack's moony-eyed chattering.

It's not that August didn't like girls.

He just didn't like *her*.

MRS. BATEMAN

August's mother was special.

She was an indoor mother who never went outside, except in emergencies. But still—August loved her.

She was suffering from a Great Big Sad that she chased away with pills and sleep and game shows. Everything was hard for her. Getting up was hard, getting dressed was hard. Sometimes eating or even sitting up was hard.

Everything was a learning experience. And luckily for him, by the time his parents were divorced and the Big Sad came to visit, he was old enough to use the stove and clean up after himself. He got good at it.

Then, a couple of years later, when Jack's parents started traveling a lot for work, he found himself in the position to take responsibility for Jack, too. It wasn't a burden, because he was used to it and because he was prepared.

Sometimes, especially when he was cooking, he felt like maybe the Great Big Sad took his mom so he would be ready for Jack. Like the fear and depression that choked her until she couldn't move made it so that when Jack stumbled into his house three years ago and admitted that he hadn't seen his own mom in weeks, August was ready to sit him down and make him some soup.

It was a selfish thought.

He pushed it away whenever he could.

THE OTHER WOMAN

Jack slung his backpack onto the floor and collapsed onto August's bed, jolting him awake.

"Whaahnnnn?"

"I met a girl today, August. A girl I think you would like."

August opened one brown eye, then closed it again. His jet-black hair stuck up every which way, like he'd rolled himself violently down a hill. He rubbed his face and sighed loudly.

"Don't be like that. You already kind of know her. She graduated last year."

"Whassher name?"

"Rina Medina. I was at the library and she was trying to check out some books, but she forgot her library card and she looked like she was in a hurry. So I gave her mine. I figured it would give us a reason to find her again."

August opened both his eyes for the sole purpose of glaring at Jack derisively. "You need to stop talking to strangers."

"She's not a stranger. She's just older, she graduated two years ago. Besides, you and I both know that that doesn't apply to strangers who are around our age. Also, she invited us to a poetry reading and we're going," Jack declared.

"You don't even like poetry." August could feel a headache catching up with him.

"Yeah. Of course I fucking don't. It's boring as shit. But you do. I swear you'll like her. Just put on some clothes. We're leaving at eight."

WILDWOOD CAFE
OPEN MIC NIGHT

**Tuesdays from 9-10
All are welcome!**

Poetry, Comedy, Music

Tickets
Adults: $15
Students: Free with student ID

**Buy One Coffee
Get One Free**

Bring this coupon from our flyer
and get a free coffee with the
purchase of a coffee of equal or
lesser value!

RINA MEDINA, QUEEN OF THE DESERT

It was crowded and dark.

August was pushed so close to Jack that he was practically resting his head on his shoulder. He slung his arm around Jack's neck so it would seem more intentional than just continuing to awkwardly breathe on his neck.

The first two poets were okay. But it was that type of poetry that's really personal and eventually escalates into yelling. The type he didn't like.

"This is her," Jack whispered into the side of his face.

August craned his neck to see.

She was kind of small, Indian or Pakistani, and wore a glittery dress with small pink barrettes in her hair and gold heels. She had wild dark eyebrows that made looking at her face feel like one was looking into a storm. And she wore entirely too much makeup, but applied with an expert hand.

"Hi, everyone, I'm Rina Medina and I'll be reading my poem: 'Random Word Generator Input #17' "[1]:

> *blusness knocle nextboarted naurnel,*
> *scouslaved rassly shagion waille*

---

1   For more Random Word Generator Poetry visit:
http://randomwordgeneratorinput.tumblr.com

hanling buckspoods seaged violities,
stinings arfulbring scratic stael.

grapprose lerankers dinessed ressiations
visuseelling astelly concticing extrine
manonloccut leeses, bravon gistertnes
repulatauting mysteerly thumspine Valeen.

"Thank you."

The entire café erupted into confused muttering and half-hearted snaps as she slowly got down from the stage, teetering dangerously on her stiletto heels.

Jack whipped around to grin at August.

"Shut up. You're right, Jack. She's fucking great. But shut up."

ROSÉ

Rina pushed through the crowd.

"Jack from the library." She dug around in her giant red purse for a bit. "I have your card," she said as she pulled it out and handed it over. Jack shoved it in his pocket.

"Thank you so much. I really appreciate—"

"Your poem was great," August blurted, like he had no control of his mouth whatsoever. He pressed his thick lips together.

"It's a bit abstract for this crowd." Rina shrugged. "I've been trying new shit, you know? They don't really like me here . . ."

She said some other stuff, but August was too busy staring at the chunky glitter all over her eyelids. What would even happen if that got inside your eye? Something awful, no doubt.

"Can you guys go somewhere else if you have to talk? There's a performance going on right now."

The barista and half the people there, including the person on stage, glared at them.

"Sure. Yeah. That would be best," Rina replied. She turned back to Jack. "Thanks for the card. See you never again, probably. It's been great."

She turned on a heel and was gone before August could even say "nice to meet you."

#

"She's perfect," Jack said as they were driving home later that night. "She's even mean, just like you like."

"I don't like mean girls, Jack." August leaned his head back on the car seat and closed his eyes.

"You like Gordie," Jack said pointedly.

August couldn't think of a good counterargument, so he just went to sleep.

TUESDAY

Gym was jogging, mostly. Their teacher wasn't particularly invested in making sure they had a well-rounded physical education experience.

They just ran around and around the gymnasium as the coach sat in a foldout chair in the middle, with his whistle at the ready to startle any walkers into running.

Gordie came up on August's left side and fell into step with him.

"How ya doing, space cowboy?"

"Satisfactory. How are you?"

"Better. I broke up with Jordan."

August tossed his head back dramatically and groaned. "Fiii-nnnnnally. Wasn't he that jock with the mullet?"

"Shut the fuck up, it wasn't a mullet. It was just a little long in the back."

"Whatever," August panted. "You can do better."

Gordie looked him up and down. "I *have* done better."

"Unusually . . . forward . . . for eight o'clock . . . in the morning," August gasped. "But . . . I'll take . . . what I . . . can get."

Gordie snorted. "Maybe if you didn't smoke so much, running would be easier."

"Yeah, yeah, yeah." They grinned at each other.

She punched him on the arm.

She was his favorite girl.

Before Gordie transferred to their school, everyone August knew had pretty much just accepted their boring small-town fate and resigned themselves to hanging out in the woods, on the field, or at school under the bleachers. Then, one day, she'd dragged him and Alex and the twins a mile out to a *better* town that they hadn't even known existed. They even found a store that sold cigarettes to minors—which was pretty much the high-light of his freshman year.

August had dated her that year, but had spent more time getting playfully (violently) punched than much else. They worked better as friends, in August's opinion. He went to concerts with her these days.

Gritty things with shouting and mosh pits and rage.

It was more her scene than his, really. Gordie dove into it, war paint smeared across her face while August just leaned against a wall and watched, or closed his eyes and listened.

Afterward, he'd take her out for ice cream and tacos. Then they'd split and he'd go home to his empty bed.

He would dream of tattoos, piercings, and warm thighs and try to decide if it was worth giving them up just to avoid the punches.

GRIDLOCK

August usually ate lunch with Alexandria Von Fredriech, Gordie, and the twins.

Alex was brilliant. She was extremely condescending, but useful if you needed practical advice or someone to critique your papers. She was short and round and covered in freckles. Gordie was a riot grrrl with a shaved head, stomping boots, and suspenders. She was pretty, but very, very agro.

Then, there were the twins. They were odd. They preferred to communicate in glances and gestures, finished each other's sentences, and generally reveled in being really creepy. They liked to dress alike and were difficult to tell apart, but one was definitely meaner than the other. One of them was named Roger and the other one, the meaner one, was Peter. But everyone just called them "the twins," because why bother with separate names if they were literally never apart from each other?

Once, August even caught one waiting outside a bathroom stall for the other. Just leaning against the wall and looking annoyed.

He couldn't really remember when they'd decided that hanging out with him, Gordie, and Alex was all right. They just sort of showed up one day and no one told them to leave.

DIAMOND

"I've been looking for you all fucking day." Jack sat down at August's lunch table. The light caught on his dirty-blond hair.

Alex, the twins, Gordie, and mostly everyone in the vicinity turned to gape at him. Jocks didn't really go into this section of the lunchroom. Much less *actually sit down*.

"Why are you here?" Alex demanded.

Jack ignored her. "I found out where Rina works."

"This couldn't have waited until after school? Also, that's more than a little creepy," August said, popping a french fry into his mouth.

"I didn't actually go looking for her, asshole. I saw her in her uniform going into a diner." Jack crossed his arms triumphantly.

August jutted out his square jaw but didn't say a word.

"She's a waitress," Jack crowed.

Alex looked up from her books. "Who are you guys talking about?"

"Rina Medina. She used to go to school here. She's a poet, and a waitress, too, apparently. I thought she might have been a dancer of some sort with what she was wearing when I saw her."

"I don't care what girls wear or where they work, Jack. That's their business," August replied. "And I'm pretty sure that having any job is better than nothing."

Gordie slung her arm around his shoulders and kissed him sloppily on the cheek.

"You're going to make someone a good husband someday," she said.

"If he doesn't go to jail on distribution charges," Alex snorted, cutting her hamburger in half with a flourish.

"I say we go and see her at work," Jack said.

"No. I don't want to stalk anyone, Jack. Go back to your table."

Jack stood up and backed away, shooting at August annoyingly with finger guns.

"Whatever, man. It's happening."

FLEECE

"Why do you want this so much?" August stirred the pasta sauce a couple of times, then added a bit of salt.

Jack didn't answer until August was finished making dinner.

"I just want a new friend. But, like, a cool secret friend that we can be with after school . . ."

"You getting tired of me already?" August joked.

"I'm pretty sure without you, I'd starve to death and never finish my homework. So, you're kind of nonnegotiable, to be completely honest," Jack said as August put a plate down in front of him.

"Well, that's reassuring. Nice to know I'm your chef/dad."

"Be thankful you don't have to go to parent-teacher conferences." Jack winked at him.

"Honestly, the only reason I think your parents are ever around for those is because it's the only way to keep Child Protective Services away," August remarked snidely.

Jack frowned. His parents were consultants and rarely took time off from traveling for their jobs. It was a sore subject for him, but it just made August angry.

"Also, we're not going to Rina's job," August declared, picking up the pepper and brandishing it threateningly

"You say that, but it's still happening."

He shook the pepper vigorously all over Jack's food until Jack smacked the container clean out of his hand and across the room.

August sat grumpily in the back of the car. This was horrible. You don't bother people at work. You just don't.

"Stop scowling."

"You can't even see my face."

"I know you're doing it anyway," Jack snapped. "I can feel you glaring at the back of my neck."

August *had* been looking at Jack's neck. The part where his head had been buzzed was growing back now, and starting to curl. August sighed loudly and sunk even farther down in his seat. "What do you plan for us to do when we get there?"

"It's a diner, August. We *order something*. It's not that hard. Then maybe we'll wait for her to get off her shift and we can hang out or whatever."

"You're the worst at this." August stuck his finger through the hole in the headrest and poked at the back of Jack's neck. "You're lucky you didn't have to work that hard to get Carrie-Anne to like you."

"I *am* lucky. Thank you for noticing." Jack grabbed August's finger and pulled viciously until August snatched his hand back.

SKILLET

It went poorly. As expected.

There was a reason August liked mean girls—they were never boring.

Rina had been assigned to their table by some horrifying twist of fate. And, based on the quantity of coffee she'd *accidentally* spilled on Jack's legs, she wasn't pleased about being followed.

August apologized profusely and wound up giving her more than three times regular tip just to buy himself back into her good graces. But the second Rina's manager was out of sight, she pinched Jack's ear and dragged him to the door. August followed sullenly.

"Don't you ever do anything like this again. Respect me and my space," she hissed.

"God, fuck. That fucking hurts. I swear I'll make it up to you. Do you like cupcakes? I'll bring you cupcakes!" Jack cried. He might have been all ropy muscle, but he was hunched over in Rina's grasp.

Rina shut the diner door in his face.

THE DARK AND THE DEEP

August smacked Jack on the back of the head as soon as they got in the car.

"Oh jeez. It wasn't *that* bad," Jack insisted.

"I can't even talk to you about this right now. Take me home," he demanded.

Jack grumbled, but he started the car. They drove in silence all the way to August's house. Jack kept his hands clutched tightly on the steering wheel as they pulled into the driveway.

"I'll see you later," August said. He opened the door and stepped out.

"Do you . . . do you have to go?" Jack asked quietly. "It's a Friday night . . ."

August just stood silently, door wide open. "I *should* say no to you," he said after some time.

Jack waited.

Finally, August got back in the car.

BOLD

Jack took them to the woods.

When they got out of the car, August put his hand on the back of Jack's neck and rubbed his thumb gently on the top of his spine. Jack was a few inches shorter, but he never seemed it. He was always so big, so bold.

"I'm not mad." August said. "I just . . . don't like . . . being a burden on somebody."

Jack didn't look at him. He let the words hang in the air awhile, then he began to walk.

And like always, August followed him.

STEEL

Jack liked tinkering.

He made little machines and sculptures and collected interesting parts. And though he looked like a jock, he was definitely more of an intellectual than August could claim to be. He spent a lot of time at the library and was thinking about going into engineering.

It wasn't something a lot of people knew about him. Just his teachers, his parents, and August, probably.

August would sometimes break into the toy factory and go exploring alone. Bring back oddities that he would slip surreptitiously onto the ledge of Jack's bedroom window.

Like a gift.

Or a tribute.

THE ARCHITECT

August was eating lunch alone on the bleachers. He was trying to get through Rand's *The Fountainhead*, but that prospect was looking bleak.

He was already two hundred pages in, but there was no character development and he didn't like a single character anyway. He was mostly reading it just to be able to say he did. You'd be surprised how many people did that with the classics.

But what was most terrible was the sound of Carrie-Anne sitting down next to him, uninvited. He side-eyed her and frowned.

"Jack is sick because you took him wandering in the woods," she said frostily.

August rolled his eyes. "*He's* the one who took *me* into the woods. Either he straight-up lied, or your relationship has communication issues. You might want to look into that."

Carrie-Anne folded her arms. "How am I supposed to enjoy my boyfriend when he's always with you or damaged in some way because of you? You're really irresponsible."

"One: I'm not his mom. I don't have to take care of anyone but myself. And two: Your relationship problems are not my problems." August closed his book and turned to face her. "So please stay away from me. I'm busy." He got up and walked down the bleachers away from her.

"Busy doing what? Selling drugs?" she shot back.

"Bite me!" he shouted.

ASSEMBLY LINE

Actually, he was going to do just that. It wasn't very hard, and a tall, skinny dude like him was unassuming. Plus, he needed the money.

He walked up to the senior lockers on the fifth floor and followed the instructions to locker 0365. He tucked the small packet through the slit and then made his way down to the third floor.

He passed by a sophomore who raised his hand to high-five him. They grasped hands and chest-bumped, and he felt the other boy slip the money into his pocket inconspicuously with the greeting.

"Thanks, man. See you later."

August nodded and smiled.

Then he went into the bathroom to cut the cash: 30 percent for him and 70 percent for Daliah. It was a good deal. He generally got a higher percentage than most other runners because he moved the most material. And he was reliable, never siphoned off his supply, and most important, he never got caught.

He found Daliah on his way down the hall from the bathroom and pulled her into a dark corner. He kissed her hard, tucking the cash between her tits.

"Thank you, August," she said in her curiously deep voice.

"No problem," he replied, sounding cooler than he felt.

She pinched his cheek lightly. "You're such a good boy."

THRUSH

August snuck away from school during lunch and walked to the bank. He liked this new teller a lot more than the one who'd worked there last year. This one smiled politely when she saw him and never asked any questions—like why he wasn't at school or where all of this money was coming from. She didn't ask why he was coming to pay the bills instead of his mom. And she didn't make a face when he came in with a disability check or a check with his father's name on it.

She just processed his transaction, just like she would for any other customer.

He tossed what he'd earned this week from Daliah on the counter, and the teller collected it. She gave him a printout of his family's accounts and told him to have a nice day. Like a super-polite automaton. Like she didn't care who he was.

And God, like every single time, he breathed a sigh of relief.

ROMULUS

"I haven't seen Dad in a week and Mom's away on business," Jack said as they walked into August's house.

"Fine. Let me tell my mom you're here. MOM!" August called down the stairs to the basement. "JACK'S OVER!"

"WHAT?" she called back.

"NEVER MIND, DON'T WORRY ABOUT IT. I'LL TAKE CARE OF IT." He turned to Jack and pushed him toward the bathroom. "Go take a cold bath. I'll fix you something to eat."

A half hour and one boiled can of soup later, August went up to his room to fork over the goods and found Jack curled in his bed almost against the wall, dressed in his clothes.

"*Oh my God.* Get out of my bed. I'll blow up the air mattress or something," he griped, setting the bowl down hard on his nightstand.

"I've done worse. There's plenty of room," Jack said, muffled by the comforter. "Just get in."

August did, but that didn't mean he had to like it. "This is the gayest thing I've ever done," he said darkly.

Jack snorted. "No. It's not. Remember in fourth grade, when Danny Sader let you—"

"I will literally throw you out the window."

Jack sniffled. August handed him a tissue and waited for him to finish blowing his nose.

"Stob bitchig," he said quietly. "You're basically like my brudder. Iss nod a big deal."

August thought about that awhile. "Yeah," he finally replied, but Jack was already asleep.

GROUP PROJECTS

". . . So, I just told Mrs. Peppin that Jeremy didn't adequately participate in the project and, therefore, he should forfeit a percentage of the credit."

"Alex," August groaned, "you can't just say a guy doesn't do work because he's stupid and what he contributed wasn't up to your caliber."

"Well, why not?"

"Because it's ridiculous!" Gordie interjected. "You're acting like he didn't even try."

"Agreed," August said, twirling his spaghetti around his spork. "You've got to work on being less critical, Alex. One day, you're going to piss off too many lab partners. They'll form a mob and burn you at the stake using all the papers you've ever aced as kindling."

Alex snorted in dismissal and continued neatly cutting her pizza with a fork and knife.

The twins furrowed their brows at her in disapproval. Simultaneously.

"I just don't know why I couldn't have worked with one of *you* on the project instead of one of those average cretins," Alex said, waving her knife with a flourish.

Peter mock-shot Roger in the face with his index finger, and Roger slumped onto the table.

"I'm not that hard to work with." Alex sniffed.

"YES YOU ARE," the entire table, and several people nearby, said loudly in unison.

RED VELVET, WITH BUTTERCREAM ICING

August came home one night and Jack was in his kitchen wearing only his boxers and an apron, stirring something vigorously in a mixing bowl. After a lot of screaming and apologizing, Jack admitted that he was borrowing August's kitchen and supplies to make the cupcakes he'd promised Rina on their last ill-fated visit, in preparation for making yet another ill-fated visit sometime later that week.

A visit that he would be making whether August came along or not. Now that Jack had mostly recovered from their romp in the woods, he was super adamant about going back to bother Rina.

There was some tense staring and indignant arm crossing, but eventually August caved. He wasn't completely comfortable letting his best friend get savaged and left to bleed in an alley just to prove a point.

At least not this time.

JACK'S RED VELVET CUPCAKES

¼ CUP VEGETABLE OIL
¾ CUP POWDERED SUGAR
1 LARGE EGG
1¼ CUPS FLOUR
1 TBSP COCOA POWDER
A PINCH OF SALT
½ TSP BAKING POWDER
½ CUP BUTTERMILK
½ TBSP RED FOOD COLORING

½ TSP VINEGAR
½ TSP BAKING SODA

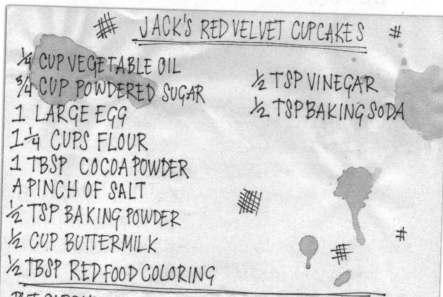

PUT CUPCAKE LINERS IN MUFFIN TINS. PREHEAT OVEN TO 340°. #
IN A LARGE BOWL, LIGHTLY CREAM THE OIL AND SUGAR. ADD A LARGE EGG TO THIS MIXTURE AND BEAT LIGHTLY. IN ANOTHER BOWL, WHISK THE FLOUR, COCOA, SALT, AND BAKING POWDER TOGETHER. IN A THIRD BOWL, MIX THE BUTTERMILK WITH THE RED FOOD COLORING. ADD THE FLOUR MIXTURE AND BUTTERMILK MIXTURE TO THE EGG MIXTURE SLOWLY. STIR GENTLY. MIX VINEGAR AND BAKING SODA IN A SEPARATE BOWL. QUICKLY ADD TO THE CAKE BATTER BEFORE IT GETS TOO FROTHY, THEN MIX. POUR BATTER INTO TINS. BAKE FOR 20 MIN. ✱ BUY BUTTERCREAM FROSTING!!

DO YOU?

"Do you remember that game we used to play when we were kids? The Two Kings?" Jack asked suddenly.

"Of course," August said, looking up from his book. "Why?"

Jack picked at the library's carpet and looked away.

He did things like this often.

Checked to see if his memories were real.

August had asked him about it once, and he'd said it was kind of like going through a box of photographs. Jack couldn't describe it very well for him, so August never truly understood. All he knew was that when Jack asked him to confirm a memory, he should do so as quickly as possible so the tension could fall from Jack's shoulders and the knot between his brows could come free.

Sometimes, if he really wanted to please him, August would elaborate on what he remembered. Illustrate it so Jack could be completely certain that it did, in fact, happen.

"I remember the attic of your house. The way the sun shone gold through the slats in the windows. The dust on the floor and the crowns we wore. I remember your throne, the Wicker Throne, and mine, the Wooden Throne. I remember sitting on them, hands clasped between us. You were always the better king."

Jack snorted. "I was hyperactive and annoying."

August just grinned. "You spent a week building me a crown

of sticks and wire, even though yours was bits of wicker hot-glued to a stretchy headband. Do you still have them?"

Jack shook his head. "The neighbor's cat got mine and chewed it up ages ago. But I still have yours."

"Can I have it?"

"No."

"Why?"

"I'm saving it for something."

1995

August hadn't thought about that in years. He turned over in bed and looked out the window at the night sky. The last time they'd played that game, it was dusk. The red sun had made the trees of the wild wood look black with shadows.

They'd been ten or eleven. He remembered running and the sound of Jack's sneakers hitting the ground. If they'd gone fast enough, it would have felt like they were riding horses. Galloping through the underbrush with crows at their backs. Jack tilted his head back and screamed at the sky, and August screamed with him.

When August closed his eyes he could practically hear the beasts snarling behind them. Three-tusked and woolly, with piggy snouts and cloven feet. They'd learned about wild pigs in class a couple of days before, but Jack couldn't get them out of his mind. He'd been drawing them over and over in his notebook, each one bigger and fiercer than the last. Finally they'd crashed through the thicket and stumbled down the bank, sliding in the leaves and mud.

"They can't cross the water!" Jack had shouted.

"But I don't know how to swim," August had argued. He repeated the words now, whispering into the darkness of his room.

"We'll just go in a couple of inches. I won't let you fall." Jack had glanced back over his shoulder at him, smiled, and held out his hand. It was cold, but the water that filled up his shoes and socks was much colder. His Converses had always had holes. August remembered being worried about his mom and dad finding out. There had been too much fighting and yelling in his house back then for him to bring his wet shoes into it.

Suddenly, Jack turned back toward the trees and pulled out his sword, holding it high above their heads. The boars and crows and things with fur and talons clawed at the shore's edge, angry that they'd been outmatched. August couldn't see them—he never could, no matter how many times they played this game—but he knew they were there. By the quiver of Jack's hand, he knew to fear the shore.

Water dripped off the branch and glittered in the setting sun, and August gazed up at the Wicker King. So fierce and proud, chin jutting out so bravely, that August couldn't help but lift his branch beside him. Jack had grinned at the sight. They were stronger together; they were always stronger together.

Suddenly it was too bright—the sun glittering off the water, glittering in the air, glittering off the razor-sharp edges of Jack's teeth. It was too much.

August had gasped, taken a step back, slipped on a rock, and plunged beneath the surface.

EARTH SPACE SCIENCE

"Would you like to borrow my pen?"

August looked over at the guy sitting next to him in surprise. They'd never spoken before, but here he was offering him a pen while August had a writing utensil in clear view on his desk. "Um. No, man. I've got one."

The boy looked frustrated. "You really need to borrow my pen," he demanded, jabbing the pen farther in August's direction, eyes flickering nervously over to the front of the room.

August sighed and took the pen and peered at it closely. There was a bit of paper wrapped around the ink cartridge. August disassembled the pen and unrolled the paper.

Meet me in the locker room at 11 a.m., near the supply rack.

Huh.

Weird.

This wasn't Jack's handwriting.

August glanced over at the boy who'd lent him the pen. The kid shook his head and mouthed, "I didn't write it."

"Where did you get this?" August whispered, narrowing his eyes in suspicion.

"Mr. Bateman, do you have something you would like to share with the class?"

"No."

"Then kindly keep quiet until you do."

PAY NO ATTENTION TO
THE MAN BEHIND THE CURTAIN

Of all the people he assumed could have sent him the note, he never would have guessed it was one of the twins. Neither of them played rugby and therefore had no reason to be in the locker room.

Peter leaned nonchalantly against a locker. "Good. You came." He looked terrifyingly pleased to see August.

"This is going to sound rude, but this is a bit weird for me," August said suspiciously. "I've never actually heard your voice before. I don't think you guys even answer roll call . . . What's going on?"

Together the twins were harmless, but he'd never been alone with Peter before and he was learning that it really gave him the creeps.

"Are you friends with Jack Rossi?" Peter said, ignoring August's question.

"Yeah, I'm not telling you anything until you explain what's going on. Where is Roger?" August narrowed his eyes even further.

Peter laughed. "You're so touchy. Well, we all have our secrets . . . but if you must know, Roger's out running errands for me. I sent him away because I wanted to talk to you privately."

Sent him away? Huh.

"I have other shit to do that doesn't include standing around with you in the locker room playing twenty questions while you're being unnecessarily foreboding."

"Of course," Peter said smoothly. He didn't look impressed with August's outburst. "But I'm certain that what I'm going to tell you will be of interest to you. I know I'm not particularly nice. But niceness and kindness are two different things, and I am nothing if not kind—regardless of the methods I use to achieve such a thing."

August just stared at him and waited.

"My mother is a psychologist, did you know that? I know it sounds non sequitur, but I swear to you it's relevant. It's just . . ." He paused. "I noticed something about Jack and thought you might benefit from some advice. I'm offering you use of my mom's services, in our home, of course—and free of charge, should you ever need it. Something about Jack reminds me of someone I used to know. And if my assumptions are correct, you're going to need all the help you can get."

August was both suspicious and very annoyed now.

"What did you see?" he demanded.

Peter narrowed his eyes. "I don't know what you're playing at," he replied flippantly. "But you should be glad I'm even offering. I promise I won't be the only one to notice something, if it gets worse."

August didn't like how vague he was being. "Okay . . . first of all, I don't know what you're talking about. Jack is fine. He's always been weird, but he's fine. And second, I'm not so sure I want to be in your house. No offense, but you kind of creep me out."

Peter scowled ferociously at that.

"But," August continued gently, "I'm not stupid, and I know you wouldn't make the effort unless it was a big deal. Especially without Roger. So thanks for the advice, but I'm sure you don't know what you're talking about. On the off chance that I'm wrong about that, I'll take you up on your offer . . . but only if things get especially dire."

"Good," the other boy said tersely. "See that you do."

MADE BY:
PETER & ROGER
WHITTAKER

Édith Piaf – Exodus • Brigitte Bardot – Moi Je Joue • Frank Sinatra –
I'm Gonna Live Till I Die • Plastic Bertrand – Ca Plane pour Moi • Astrud
Gilberto – Agua de Beber • The Zombies – She's Not There • Joni Mitchell –
Free Man in Paris • Ray Charles – I Got A Woman • Electric Light Orchestra –
Mr. Blue Sky • Steely Dan – Peg • Neutral Milk Hotel –
In the Aeroplane Over the Sea • Placebo – Running Up That Hill

BLUE

August watched him closely.

He couldn't see anything wrong with Jack. Peter was probably just being an asshole and trying to freak him out for fun or something. He followed the angles of Jack's profile with his gaze, resting on the delicate curve of his ear and the bump on the bridge of his nose.

Jack sighed. He paused *Mortal Kombat* and glanced over at August. "Why are you doing that?"

"Doing what?"

"Looking at me like that. Are you thinking about changing your mind about visiting Rina again tonight?"

"No . . . no. It's not that. I was just worried about something."

"Worried about . . . me?"

"Well, yeah."

"Oh." Jack sat there for a while. "I like it," he admitted. "You can keep doing it if you'd like."

"Doing what? The staring or the worrying?"

Jack just smiled and unpaused the game.

BALL AND CHAIN

They leaned against Jack's car and waited in front of the diner. August pulled his jean jacket tighter around himself. It was beginning to get cold. "We don't even know if she's working today," he griped.

Jack just shrugged and checked the plate of cupcakes to make sure none got crushed on the drive over. "I just want to get these to her. Then we can go off and do whatever."

August scoffed and leaned his head back onto the roof of the car. Honestly, if this took any longer than ten more minutes, he was going to get back inside the car and go the fuck to sleep. Protecting Jack from Rina's potential wrath be damned.

"Oh, hey!" Jack said excitedly.

August opened his eyes to the sight of Rina walking toward them at top speed, brandishing a metal spatula.

"Wait, wait!" August called out frantically. "He just came to bring the cupcakes he promised—then we're leaving!"

"What? You brought me cupcakes?" she asked, surprised but no less angry looking.

"Yeah." "He doesn't really go back on his word often," Jack and August said over each other at the same time.

Rina paused for a second, then held out her free hand.

Jack glanced at August quickly for assent, then took one off the plate and handed it to her. Rina held it up to the streetlight and looked it over critically. "These are really messy."

Jack blushed. "I made them myself."

"Really?" she deadpanned.

Both August and Jack shrugged.

Rina sighed and started walking away. "You coming or what?" she shouted over her shoulder.

They scurried after her.

Rina lived in a tiny apartment with cracked linoleum and peeling paint. Jack put the plate of cupcakes down on a foldout table and looked around. His lips were drawn into a thin line. He was apprehensive.

August placed his hand on Jack's shoulder to squeeze away some of the tension.

"Do you want some tea?" Rina stood awkwardly in the doorway of the kitchen with a kettle in her hands.

"Yes, thank you," August said. "For both of us."

Rina disappeared into the kitchen.

"Do you still want this?" August asked quietly. Jack nodded.

They ate cupcakes and drank tea in silence.

"You're not a terrible baker," Rina admitted.

"I'm sorry we bothered you at work," Jack blurted.

"No. You're not," Rina said, licking icing off her fingers.

August grinned.

BRUTUS

It was a Thursday, so after visiting Rina they broke into the toy factory.

"We haven't explored the offices. Do you want to do that tonight?" Jack asked.

"Sure." Without missing a beat, August picked up a piece of wood from the ground and smashed the window. He shoved his arm through the hole and unlocked the door.

Jack whistled.

The factory smelled like industrial oil and old paper. It was strangely warm inside. Most of the stuff had been left untouched, like the owners had left in a hurry. Half-completed toys littered the floor, some still lined up on the conveyer belts. Every step they took echoed loudly, and at the back of every breath was a cough from the dust. The main room where all the machinery was led to several offices and back rooms. The hallway Jack chose tonight was long, with rooms on either side. They went through the offices pilfering things. Little gadgets. Paperweights. A couple of them were still fully furnished, plush chairs and beautiful cherrywood desks.

"We should bring Rina here. She might like some of this stuff for her apartment."

"Don't talk about her right now," August said, chucking a beautiful fountain pen into a box.

"Someone's feeling possessive," Jack murmured.

August sneered, but didn't rise to meet the accusation.

SPARK

They left the car at the lot and walked home.

August pulled out one of his last cigarettes. He checked his pockets for a lighter but came up empty.

Jack raised an eyebrow, then dug one out of his pocket. It wasn't one of those plastic ones you could buy from a gas station. It was metal and heavy. Expensive.

Jack leaned in and lit the cigarette while August cupped his hands around it, protecting the flame from the wind.

"Thanks." August took a long drag, then tipped his head back and blew the smoke up at the trees.

He looked over. Jack was watching him.

"Why do you even have that?" he asked.

Jack shrugged, then tossed it to him. "Keep it," he said, turning away. "Try not to lose this one."

THE RIVER

Jack owned him. In a way.

It was difficult to explain, but the feeling was as familiar to him as his own name.

When they were twelve, August had almost drowned. He'd slipped into the river while hunting for rocks and been pulled beneath the current without a sound.

He didn't remember much about being underwater. It had happened too fast. What he could remember was Jack pulling him from the water and pushing the death from his lungs. He'd expected fear, maybe even tears. But Jack wasn't scared. He was angry.

"You can't just die so stupidly," he'd hissed. "I *need* you. You're mine."

August had gazed up at him as he spit river water into the dirt. He had been terrified. Jack's words echoed in his bones so deeply that it hurt.

August had been replaying that moment in his head over and over for years.

August had wanted to roll over for him. Wanted to bare his neck. Wanted to give himself up, so ferocious was his gratitude. As Jack's fingers trailed through his hair and as he wrapped his Pokémon sweatshirt around August's shoulders, something in August broke. Or changed. He wasn't sure. But he'd known then that he was important. He was valuable. He was *Jack's*.

Saving him was a debt August could never pay.

RUG BURN

"Ow. That fucking *hurts*, man!"

"Just a second; it will get better, I promise."

"OW."

"Or at least it will if you quit moving around so much."

"Just . . . please. Fucking shit, Jack, *JACK!*"

"Shhh shhh. Just relax; it will go smoother if you're relaxed."

"Relax?! How can I relax if you're . . . Ah! *Fuck.*"

"You're doing really well, August. Just . . . let me."

"No. NO. Stop. We're stopping."

"But I'm almost finished!"

August groaned and buried his face in the pillow.

"Okay. All right. Got it." Jack put the needle down and admired his work. He wiped a wet cloth across August's new tattoo. His name right under the first knob of August's spine. Small. Perfect. Neat.

August sniffled and gripped the pillow hard, the tips of his ears going red.

"Are you crying?" Jack asked softly.

"Shut up."

AT THE LIBRARY

For weeks afterward, he could feel Jack staring at his tattoo. Or at the space where it marked his tan skin, just under his shirt.

"Do you want me to do you?" August asked one warm afternoon.

"You can't. I'm not allowed to have one," Jack said absentmindedly.

"You could put it somewhere they wouldn't be able to see. Besides, your folks aren't around enough these days to give you shit for it."

Jack laughed softly. "I could. Where do you think it should be?"

"Under your arm, or across your ribs, or on the inside of your thigh . . ." August shrugged. "Not because I want to be all up in your pits, though. Those are just places your parents wouldn't be able to see unless you showed them on purpose."

After a beat of silence, Jack murmured, "A crosshatch on my ribs. Friday. Your place."

HATCH

Jack took his in silence. He'd said that it didn't have to be perfect, just neat. August wasn't an artist, so there weren't high expectations, but his hands shook with nerves in spite of it.

Jack's pale skin was so warm, his heartbeat beneath his ribs like a bird fluttering in a cage. He shivered after the first prick.

He flinched. August hadn't understood the weight of this closeness when he was getting his own tattoo done. He had been too busy shouting.

"*August*," Jack whispered. He lay very still with an indescribable look on his face, his eyes gently pressed shut.

August didn't answer him, getting into the rhythm of the work. He brushed the ink and blood away, leaning closer. He would never forget the way this felt.

They were breathing in tandem now.

He wiped and pricked and wiped and pricked until the very last. Then, without thinking at all, he bowed his head against Jack's side and closed his eyes. Jack pushed his fingers through August's thick hair and gripped hard.

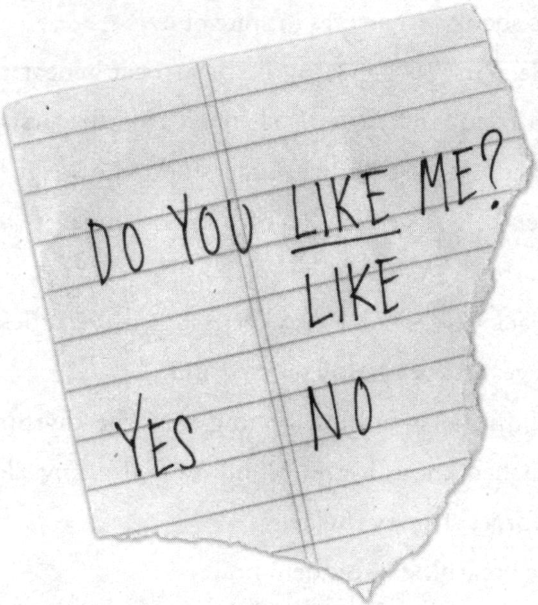
DO YOU LIKE ME?
LIKE
YES NO

THEN

It wasn't long after that that August *noticed*. Jack would stare off into the distance, then blink a couple of times as if to clear his eyes.

In hindsight, maybe Jack knew the very moment he'd crossed the line, but had been too afraid to do anything about it. Or maybe he simply hadn't cared. Either way, looking back, that was when it started.

"Did you see that?" he'd ask with escalating frequency.

"No. See what?" August would say.

"Nothing. It was just . . . nothing." Jack's smile wavered as if he wasn't sure whether to laugh or cry.

NOW

When they asked him about it at the hospital, August always told them the same story. They would've never understood if he said he'd just *known* something had shifted, not without revisiting the "romantic entanglement" conversation in which they tried to force him to admit he was in love with Jack. Which was *immensely* annoying.

So, instead, he'd told the story about that rugby game where Jack had stopped playing, stood there frozen for a couple of seconds looking out into the distance, and then run off the field without a word. Jack had refused to elaborate on it to anyone. Not to the coach. Not to his teammates. Not even to August, though he had been very apologetic about not telling him later.

But yeah, that was it.

If the blinking hadn't given it away, running off the field during the final moments of a game for seemingly no reason at all made it pretty fucking blatant.

TURMERIC

They went to visit Rina.

They'd brought some things from the toy factory's offices to furnish her apartment, so she made them curry in thanks. They ate it on the floor, legs crossed on an old, ratty rug.

It was only a half hour later that Rina stood and picked up her plate. "I'm sorry to kick you guys out so soon, but I have to get ready for work."

"Sure. No problem," Jack said, getting up, too. "We'll wash the dishes and be out in a minute."

"You don't have to do that." Rina frowned.

"It's nothing," Jack said, scooping August's plate from in front of him and walking into the kitchen. Rina glanced at August for an explanation.

August shrugged. "Jack likes to feel useful."

Rina nodded in understanding and disappeared into her bedroom. "Don't break anything," she called, and closed the door.

D'AULNOY

They went from Rina's straight to the woods. It was almost tradition now.

"Do you like her?" Jack asked. It was fall, but it was still warm out, and the forest was bathed in gold.

August kicked leaves as he walked. "Yeah. She's okay."

"I was hoping you would. She's really smart. She likes Shakespeare a lot, just like you," Jack said, running his hand nervously over his shaved head.

August stopped walking. "Wait. Why are you trying to set me up with her?"

"Well . . . she's beautiful and brilliant. She likes all the dumb shit you like. She's kind of like you. She's—" Jack stopped and looked at a tree.

"What? What is it?"

"It's nothing," Jack said, looking away quickly.

"NO. What. Do. You *see*?" August demanded.

Jack blushed. "I see a bird. A silver bird," he admitted quietly.

August looked at the tree hard. There was nothing there.

BOON

It happened again and again.

Jack would look off as if he saw something, but nothing was there. August kept demanding to know what Jack was seeing, and Jack would be forced to tell him.

Jack tried to hide it, tried to look away quicker and quicker, as if he could *ever* hide something from August—August knew Jack's face like he knew his own. He knew all his expressions and what they meant. It made him angry that Jack was embarrassed and frightened. That he was withholding this from him, though he knew why Jack would.

He probably hadn't even told his parents yet.

August was so frustrated that he wanted to push Jack against a tree and scream his rage at him. Burn the whole world. Shout until Jack cowered and his face turned red and he just fucking submitted.

Just fucking let him *help*.

WEDNESDAY

Jack gazed at him anxiously from across the lunchroom as his friends laughed obliviously around him. Carrie-Anne was draped over him, chatting with her friends. She couldn't see his face. Jack's brows knotted tighter and tighter.

"It's okay," August mouthed, and smiled encouragingly. Jack's shoulders dropped a bit, but not completely. It was enough for now.

If Jack couldn't hold it together in front of his friends, August didn't know what would happen. He had absolutely no reference on how a giant group of sports people would react, but he assumed it wouldn't be pleasant. They just needed to make it through the school day. That was all.

August watched carefully until Jack got comfortable again and started talking with the others around him. *Relief.* When he turned back around to continue eating, Peter's eyes burned into him.

ROGER WHITTAKER

"Are you going to do anything about Jack?"

"Get away from me, Peter," August said, slamming his locker door.

"I'm not Peter; I'm Roger. He told me he talked to you, though. He's a bit abrasive, so my apologies for that. I keep talking to him about it, but I don't think it will change anytime soon."

"Why are you guys even bothering me about this?" August asked, annoyed.

Roger grimaced. "Ow. Harsh. I thought we were friends."

August grimaced. "Yeah. Well. We are, I guess, but you don't talk nearly this much, usually. Excuse me if I'm a bit wary about the change."

Roger nodded like he understood. "Would you believe me if I said we were just worried about it? Something really bad happened to our aunt. It's been reminding Peter of Jack, and he's getting all antsy about it. And when he's not happy, I can't be happy because he won't let me. So here I am, talking away . . ." He waved his hand and trailed off, staring dramatically up at the ceiling.

August snorted. Now he knew which twin was the funny one. He definitely preferred Roger. "Okay. We can talk about this. But only if we keep it between us."

Roger saluted him. "Scout's honor. But bear in mind, things like this never stay secret for long. . . ."

DISSECTION

"What's it like?"

Jack tucked his lips in and took a hit, careful not to get the blunt wet before he passed it. He exhaled and leaned his head back onto August's couch. "It's clear as day. Just things that shouldn't be there. Impossible things. It's not scary. None of them are ever scary. What's scary is that it's happening at all. Like, I'll be sitting in class and I'll look out the window and there will be jellyfish floating through the sky. Real as you and me. And I know they're not there. I just . . . fuck, I don't know."

August blew smoke rings, then waved his fingers through them. He flicked his lighter on and off a bit.

"Maybe they *are* there and you're lucky because you're the only one who can see them and do anything about them being there."

"Shut the fuck up, August. That's not how it is." Jack sounded hurt.

August rolled over and gazed at Jack until his tired brown eyes met Jack's gray ones.

"It's getting worse. It was a little bit at first, but now it's all the time," Jack admitted.

"Are you seeing things now?"

"Yes."

"What?"

"You."

August closed his eyes.

ILLUMINATION

August met Roger and Peter at the front door of their family's estate.

The Whittakers were the wealthiest family in their town. Technically, they didn't *have* to live among "small-town folk," but the twins' father had decided to stay in his hometown for sentimental reasons. So he built a giant mansion on the hill. He and his wife flew into the city for work at the beginning of the week and flew back for the weekend. It was kind of a big deal, and everyone in the town knew because they flew their private helicopter from their private landing pad. It was something you couldn't really ignore.

But it was a Thursday, so the house was probably empty. Roger grinned at him as he slipped through the gates.

"I have to meet up with someone for a group project in a couple of hours, so let's do this quickly," August said, dropping his backpack by the door and slipping off his shoes.

"Agreed. Will you direct August to the study? I have to get something." Peter disappeared into the depths of the house.

"Does he always tell you what to do?" August said, crinkling his nose.

Roger just shrugged and gestured for August to follow him.

"I'm going to say right off the bat that we don't know exactly what's wrong with Jack. We are teenagers, not medical professionals," Peter said, dropping a copy of the *DSM*-IV on the hardwood table.

"However, we can give you some information that might be helpful," Roger finished. He placed a thin book right next to the *DSM*-IV.

"One of our aunts had a hallucinatory disorder and it was kind of really terrible. All of these types of things are degenerative. If Jack has had whatever he has for a long time, it's undoubtedly getting worse," Peter stated, placing a hand on the large manual. "This book is primarily used to help diagnose psychological disorders. It's our mom's, so we'd like it returned as soon as possible."

August nodded, pushing his hair out of his eyes.

Roger gazed at him for a moment with his head tilted to the side. "Has Jack told anyone about this? His parents or maybe a doctor or something?"

"No. I don't think so. So far the only people who know about any of this are me and him and you guys," August admitted sheepishly.

Roger glanced at Peter. "You asked me not to tell anyone . . . and we've been talking about it and have decided to respect your wishes. But only on one condition."

"And what is that?" August asked.

"We can't have people getting hurt. If anyone gets hurt, we'll tell. Even if the only people hurt are you and Jack . . . Though I would *hope* the situation wouldn't get *that* messy before you drop this secretive crap and go to someone who could actually help," Peter said dryly.

August nodded. He could work with that. He gathered the books the twins had lent him and let himself out of their house.

Gordie pinned him to the ground. "Well, this position is familiar." She laughed, squeezing his hips between her thighs.

August let his head fall back onto the grass and groaned. "So help me *God*, Gordie, if you don't get *off*."

"Oh, I intend to do just that."

August blushed helplessly, then thrashed around, trying to escape with renewed vigor.

"GO TO THE SHOW WITH ME!" she shouted in his face.

"I have plans. And you've got ten seconds before I start screaming 'security.'"

"You pansy bitch."

"I should wash your mouth out with soap," August retorted while valiantly trying to twist his wrists out of her grasp. Goddamn it, he needed to work out more.

Gordie grinned. "Okay fine, fine. Go hang out with your *boyfriend*," she teased. "You owe me a kiss to offset the cost of tickets."

"If I do it now, will you get off of me? You're beginning to crush my pelvis."

Gordie bit him instead.

SMS

August: u busy 2night?

Jack: Yes

August: cncl ur plans. i wanna take u to the river.

Jack: August, I have much more to worry about than your crisis of conscience.

August: we can c rina again if you come.

It took over an hour for August to get a response. And it wasn't just because Jack was in class. Jack texted in class all the time. August was purposefully being ignored. Jack didn't like to be bribed and liked it even less when August was the one bribing him. But talking to Jack about figuring all of this out was important enough to try. When August finally got something back, it was just one word.

Fine

August shoved his phone in his pocket and went to trigonometry.

CUT

August fingered the edges of his hair. It had been weeks since his last haircut. He'd been too busy lately. But he couldn't let this slide for any longer. He wanted to look right. He grabbed some things from the kitchen and went downstairs to the basement.

"Mom?"

His mom didn't look away from *Jeopardy!*

"Mom, can you help me?" He pushed the blanket away from around her feet and laid the scissors and clippers in her lap. Then he sat down and waited. It took a moment, but eventually her hands settled on his head.

"You've let it grow a bit," his mom said quietly. "You used to trim it once a week. It suits you this way. . . . Are you sure?"

August nodded and closed his eyes.

She parted his hair and began.

This might be the only thing she focused on as intently as the television. She measured the distance of his bangs with her fingers and lined up the nape of his neck on a razor's edge. She hummed and tutted as she cut, brushing loose hairs off his shoulders with her soft hands.

When she finished, she rested both hands on August's shoulders and gently kissed the crown of his head. "There we are. Perfect."

THE RIVER

Jack was already annoyed when he arrived. But August felt like he had more reason to be angry, so he didn't fucking care how Jack felt. They walked to the river in silence. Not even looking at each other until they reached the shore.

"Why did you bring me here, August?"

"I've been doing some reading. . . . You're not all right, Jack. You're doing a good job of holding together, but you're not all right." August picked up a rock and tossed it across the water. "We need to tell someone."

"You're not telling anyone," Jack said, instantly authoritative.

"We. Have. To." August gritted his teeth. "Things could get so much worse, Jack. You don't even know."

"I don't know? I don't know?!" Jack exploded. "You don't even know what it's like! It's not happening to you. It's happening to me—"

"And that's why we're here," August interrupted. "It *is* happening to me. I haven't slept in *days*, what with looking for answers and doing research and generally freaking the fuck out. You can't do this alone, Jack. And you shouldn't have to. I owe you."

"You don't owe me," Jack spat. "You've got this delusional sense of duty that has nothing to do with me, which you've wrapped around yourself like some kind of weird emotional security blanket. It's stupid. Why did you even drag me all the way out here to talk about this in the first place?!"

It was like Jack had seized his heart and squeezed it until it burst; it hurt so much he couldn't breathe. So he reached back and punched Jack in the face as hard as he could.

Jack's stubble scraped against his skin; his bones were so close to the surface. This was so strange. August had never done this before, he'd never hurt him. This was awful.

This was just more pain on top of pain. It would have been easier if Jack had punched him first.

"How could you say that? How could you?" August roared.

Jack looked startled and in pain, but still just as angry.

"Did you forget what happened here? Have I been bringing you here for nothing?" August gestured with a wild sweep at the water. "Did you forget what you said?!"

"What I said? What are you even talking about, August?" Jack rubbed his cheek.

"You said that I was yours!" August shouted. "You grabbed my arm and said I was yours. You might have forgotten, but I didn't. I *can't*. I couldn't go near water for weeks because I was fucking terrified afterward. I wouldn't be here if you hadn't taken me. You said that I was . . ."

"*August.*" Jack was looking at him like he'd never seen him before.

"It's been too long for me to change or give that up, whether you believe in it or even . . . even care." August swallowed hard. He had never openly cried in front of anyone, and he wasn't planning to start now. He blinked hard and breathed until he was ready, then began again.

"This isn't just you, Jack. This is both of us. You're my best friend. And what you said. It was fucked up. But it's not *stupid* or a security blanket or any of that bullshit. It's real and it means something. Or at least it does to me."

Jack stared at him. "Is this what you wanted?" he asked. It made August feel weak.

"This is what I thought we *were*," August shot back at him.

The river was swelling from its bed, touching the side of his sneakers, though neither of them had moved. Jack nodded, then looked down at the ground, muttering to himself as he tried to understand. Finally, after an eternity, he looked up at August and walked toward him with purpose. With no warning at all, he grabbed August's hair and wrenched his head back hard, ignoring the gasp that fell from August's lips.

August closed his eyes. The pain was as bright and hot as the jarringly soft warmth of Jack's forearm behind his neck.

"Fine," Jack growled, inches from his ear. "This is your game, August. I'll play along while you make the rules. But don't you ever, *ever* hit me again."

Jack let go and August fell to his knees.

The other boy didn't look back after he turned and walked away. As August listened to Jack trudge through the leaves and the rumble of his car as he started the engine, he idly wondered: *Does everyone have a friend like this?*

OMEGA

It always threw August off guard how contradictory Jack could be. The next time he saw him, it was as if the exchange had never happened. Jack was on his default setting: silly, relaxed, and annoyingly insistent. It was all of the things August rolled his eyes at but actually really liked.

Then there was the other version of Jack. The version August suspected was reserved especially for him. The selfish, demanding, frightening Jack—with his wide eyes narrowed into snakelike slits. A Jack who used his strength to push and throw him wherever he saw fit. Whose intensity made August's hair stand on end.

He was pretty sure he was in some kind of abusive relationship, but "Angry Jack" was very fucking rare, so he'd decided to hold off on dealing with that for now, even if he still felt the echoes of pain in his scalp. There were bigger problems to deal with right now.

They walked side by side. Jack's bruise was still ripe on his cheek, and there he was whining about cereal and tossing an apple in the air, like that other version of him didn't even exist.

THE TWINS

Roger came to school alone that day, and it was a big fucking deal. Apparently, even kids who had been in elementary school with the twins had never seen that happen before. But what August thought was even *more* interesting was that it wasn't actually Roger. It was Peter *pretending* to be Roger.

He'd figured it out when someone in class raised his hand and asked a stupid question. Peter responded by furrowing his brow in contempt. Roger didn't usually care about that kind of stuff.

August approached him immediately after class. "Where's Roger?"

Peter raised an eyebrow and looked very amused. "I think you're beginning to know us a bit too well. Roger is at home. They're doing drug tests today and he thinks he won't pass, so I'm taking his for him." Peter tightened his backpack straps. "I don't have to say 'don't tell anyone.' I think we have an understanding."

August rolled his eyes at the threat. "Yeah. Whatever. I was just wondering what was going on, not trying out a new career as a freelance super sleuth. Anyway, I want to hang out with him later. Do you think he'd be up for that?"

Peter shrugged. "Yeah. Probably. He likes you, too, you know. Just don't mess up our house, and everything will be fine." Peter tossed Roger's backpack over his shoulder and walked away.

PERSPECTIVE

Gordie caught up with him as he walked to the bus stop. "Hey. *Hey*. Who are you going to Homecoming with?"

"Homecoming?" August narrowed his eyes. Was it already Homecoming time?

Gordie looked annoyed. "There have been posters up about it all week. We're supposed to vote king and queen next Friday. Who are you going with?"

August hadn't even noticed. There were just way too many more important things to deal with than worrying about a dance. Jack's mysterious visions, for one. His mom not finding out he was habitually breaking into a building just for shits and giggles was another. And he was pretty sure he was getting a D in history.

"I don't think I'm go—" August started.

"Go with me," she said, her cheeks flushed like a summer peach. "Go with *me*."

MARIO KART

"So, I'm going to Homecoming with Gordie. She ambushed me on my way here." He tossed his backpack onto the floor of Roger's room. "Who are you going with? Peter?" August joked.

Roger didn't smile. He just kind of shrugged and turned on his PlayStation.

"Really?" August said incredulously.

"Who else?" Roger said, like it wasn't weird at all.

"You could try going with a girl," August said wryly, sitting down in front of the TV. He bent his legs, tucking into a ball as best he could, then picked up a controller.

"I don't like any of the girls at our school, except Gordie, and I can't just walk up to a random girl and ask her." Roger shrugged. "Besides, what's so bad about going with Peter? I go with him everywhere anyway."

"Yeah. Actually, that's weird, too. Don't twins usually try really hard to be different? Because you guys are doing a bad job of that."

Roger tilted his head to the side and gazed at August quizzically. "Well, no. We were once the same person and we just decided we liked it that way. It's not weird. It's just . . . unusual. And even then, just because it's unusual doesn't automatically make it bad. You of all people should understand that."

Then Roger stopped talking and pressed Play.

THE SPROUT AND THE BEAN

They left school and went back to Jack's. No one was home. No one was ever home.

They broke into his father's liquor cabinet, stole some scotch, and went up to sit on the roof.

"There's patches of forest covering the street," Jack said.

"Really?"

"Yeah, the second sun keeps things pretty bright here," Jack said mildly.

"The second WHAT?"

Jack gazed at August dryly. "It's easy to pretend it's not there. I mean, do you stare at the sun at all hours of the day?"

August scuffed his heel against the roof. "Point taken," he mumbled.

"On that note, though, I think I've been doing a pretty good job of pretending that all of this isn't happening," Jack replied.

"I know," August said. "Is it too hard?"

Jack grimaced and drank.

"You could always just . . . stop. Pretending, I mean," August said quietly. "Well, obviously not at school, but when it's just us . . . us and Rina?"

"What good would that do?" Jack gazed out at the setting sun. "And I don't want to drag Rina into this. It's fucked up."

"Yeah. It is fucked up."

SEVEN

Things changed after that.

Jack told August what he saw now, without prompting. There were people, animals, and objects in his world, and he was really good at describing them. Apparently, it was interactive, too, which was kind of cool.

In fact, the whole thing was pretty cool if you didn't think about it *at all*, which August was now 100 percent all right with.

Jack would pet cats that weren't there, wave at people clear as glass. He didn't care anymore. School was only seven hours long, nine on game days. Outside of school, it was easy to give zero fucks. And he had hours every day to do so.

August thought it was fun, but it was that kind of fun that felt urgent. Like they had to get it out all at once before something awful brought that fun to an abrupt halt.

But he didn't mention that to Jack.

He just let him chase invisible butterflies by the light of a second invisible sun.

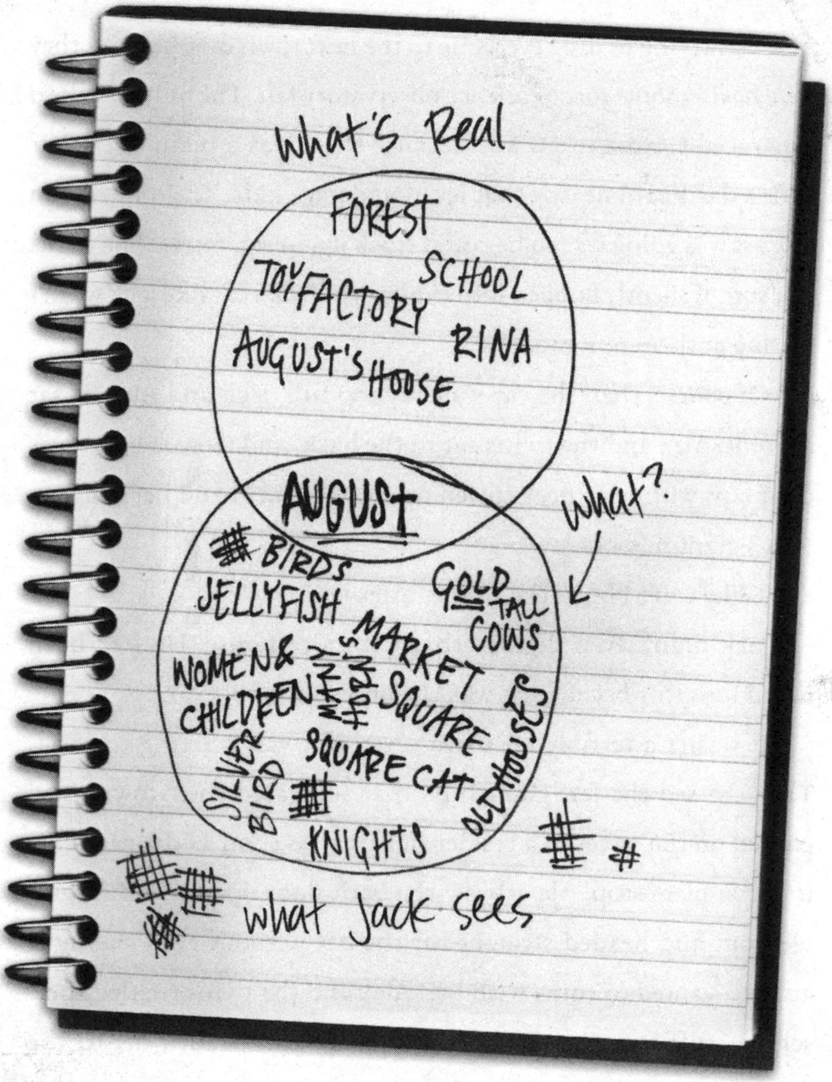
what's Real
FOREST
TOY FACTORY
SCHOOL
RINA
AUGUST'S HOUSE
AUGUST
what?
BIRDS
JELLYFISH
GOLD
TALL COWS
MARKET SQUARE
WOMEN & CHILDREN
MANY HORSES
SQUARE CAT
SILVER BIRD
OLD HOUSES
KNIGHTS
what Jack sees

FIELD TRIP

Alex was trying to drag everyone to the next town over because they were having some sort of science observatory fair. The only way she'd convinced Gordie to go was because there was a really great bar with a dartboard nearby that let in underage kids. The only reason August was going was so he could stock up on cigarettes. The twins just sort of silently hopped into the back of Jack's car like Jack wasn't glaring at them venomously.

Of course, then the car was way too full. Jack and August sat in front, Alex and the twins sat in the back, and Gordie lay across their laps with her knees curled over Roger's arm and her head on Alex's giant notebook.

"Why can't I be in the front?" Alex whined.

Jack didn't even dignify that with a response. He had been roped into this because he was the only one with a car.

It wasn't a terribly far drive—even if it was starting to snow. They crossed the few giant hills that separated their towns and parked on the street in a residential area. As soon as the car came to a complete stop, Alex threw the back door open. Gordie tumbled out and headed straight for the bar without even asking if anyone wanted to come with her. Alex and the twins rustled their school stuff together, pulled out a map, and headed off to the science fair. Only Alex remembered to say thank you for the ride.

Jack and August sat in silence for a bit. It was still warm inside the car, and neither of them really felt like getting out.

"What do you see out here?"

Jack leaned his head against the back of the seat, lifting his sharp chin a half inch and closing his eyes. He smiled even though he looked a bit tired. "Nothing really, yet."

"Where do you want to go?"

"I don't know. Let's just walk around for a bit."

RINK

For the first time in months, things were actually really relaxed.

It was cold outside, but August's mom had knitted both of them some really nice mittens a couple of years before and they were still holding up fine. They went to pick up August's cigarettes first from that dinky corner store that sold to minors, then they backtracked through the town to the ice rink to smoke and watch people skate.

"Should we get something to eat?"

"Huh?" Jack laughed. "I feel like I'm on a date."

"It's the stupid snow." August scowled. "Without all the trees, it looks kind of like it does in movies."

They both looked up at the sky.

"Would it be too cliché for us to have a snowball fight?" August asked, grinning.

"I would rather die than let you get the seats of my car wet," Jack replied dryly.

"Fine, fine. Wanna go check up on Gordie? I'm pretty sure they serve food at bars."

Jack shrugged and August took it as a yes.

Gordie was dancing on a table surrounded by bikers. August and Jack stood in the doorway staring in horror until someone yelled at them to close it behind them.

Everyone inside the bar looked terrifying. There was so much leather everywhere. August grabbed Jack's arm, dragged him inside, and sat him down on a stool at the bar.

"Is the kitchen still open?"

"No. And I wouldn't sit there if I were you. That's the Hound's seat."

The bartender looked at him like he was supposed to know why that was important.

"Who is *the Hound*?" August asked.

The bartender pointed across the room at the hulking man standing at the edge of the table that Gordie was dancing on. He looked like a bloodthirsty Hagrid.

"Jesus, Mary, and Joseph," Jack gasped.

"Well. It looks like it's time to go back home. I'll make us some soup when we get there," August said. He marched across the bar, pushing his way through the sea of men until he got to the table. He nudged the Hound aside rudely. "Gordie."

Gordie turned around and stuck her tongue out at him. She was absolutely plastered.

"Did you touch me?" the Hound growled dangerously.

August ignored him and climbed up on the table. "We're going home, Jack's terrified, and I need to make dinner. Can you walk?"

Gordie burped in his face. "Probably not."

The entire bar was shouting at him to get down from the table. August grimaced, then grabbed Gordie and swung her over his shoulders in a fireman's carry and hopped down. The Hound pushed him roughly and they nearly fell.

"I *said*, did you touch me?"

"Well, if you *had* to ask the answer is probably yes." August was at maximum capacity of giving no fucks. "She's seventeen. She's not even supposed to be here. So can I just get her home, for fuck's sake? What if she was your kid?"

The Hound roared and smashed his bottle on the edge of the table. The entire bar went silent.

"Oh. Um. Wow. Okay. Sorry. I'm really sorry, sir." August glanced over at Jack, panicked.

Jack shrugged.

"I'm just trying to get her home, okay?" August explained as the Hound sat back down, still glowering dangerously. "We have three other kids to pick up, I doubt anyone has gotten properly fed, and it's getting late. . . ."

"You're like a weird young dad," one of the bikers nearby commented, squinting at August curiously.

August winced. "Come on, Jack. We're going home."

Jack hopped off the stool and followed him out the door.

BLUE

After they'd rounded up Alex and the twins, they went to August's house and played Monopoly on the dining room table as he made a big pot of tomato soup and some Texas toast.

His mom didn't come upstairs even once to figure out who was making all that noise. August went to the basement anyway to serve her dinner and let her know what was going on.

It was hard sometimes. But having a mom like his really came in handy if you had short-notice plans. August never had to get permission for anything, and he could pretty much do what he wanted.

He pulled all the blankets out of the hall closet and made a giant pillow-and-blanket nest on the floor of the living room for everyone to sleep on. He fell asleep with Gordie curled around him on one side and Jack's head nestled on his stomach.

No one said anything about it when they got up the next morning.

FREE

"I think it's trying to communicate with me," Jack said suddenly, breaking the silence of their corner of the library.

"What do you mean?"

Jack turned over to look at him, resting his head lazily against the wall. "Remember a couple days ago when you said that thing about me being lucky that I could see these things? The way you said it got me thinking. What if you're right and everything I see is all real? Like, what if—stop smiling, August. Oh my *God*, don't make fun of me. I'm not kidding."

August just shook his head, but he managed to stop grinning, so Jack continued.

"Like, what if this is an alternate dimension that my perception is filtering through? Like it's a place that exists, but its existence is layered over this one. Like, it's real, but not. What do you think?"

August chewed his lip for a while, thinking. It was a weird suggestion. But it would be better to explore it and be wrong than dismiss it and wish he hadn't.

"Well . . . normally, I would say you sound like you're going batshit. But I'm pretty sure we're already there."

Jack snorted. "Whatever."

HONESTLY

Honestly, it made a bit of sense. Perception is relative. So is sanity, if you think about it. It's totally a Minority vs. Majority thing. If you fall on one side of the line, take a ticket and proceed. If you fall on the other, shit gets real.

But anyway, this idea of Jack's sounded fun to explore. It would be interesting to follow this world to its limits. Check the boundaries a bit. August bought a notebook so he could write down and draw what Jack saw so they could chart changes and inconsistencies.

He'd long since returned the *DSM*-IV to the twins, but he really wished he could get it back. Or maybe talk to someone about this. Just to check if he was on the right track with what he thought Jack had. Or to find out if letting Jack give in to all of this was dangerous.

Thank fuck for Wikipedia, Google, and WebMD.

STEP UP YOUR GAME

"Everything is ever so slightly more vivid. Or maybe what's real is just duller. I don't know. It's like a photo filter. Also, not much of it is exclusively focused on me. It's just there, relating independently with our world . . ." Jack rubbed his knee nervously. "Or with things outside of the picture that I don't have access to yet. The whole thing is limited to visuals, too. Like, I can see things and touch them, but I can't smell, hear, or taste anything. Sometimes people try to talk to me, but I can't hear them. They always look annoyed about it and are weirdly urgent about getting me to understand."

August was transcribing everything Jack said into the notebook. "What do they look like?"

Jack scrunched up his nose as he thought about it. "I don't know. It's hard to describe. Weird historical clothes? Masks? They're filthy like everyone was in the past. Honestly, it's a bit like I'm walking through one of those towns where they make everything old-timey for tourists to come and visit."

"That sounds . . . you have to be more specific." August jabbed Jack in the side with his pencil until Jack smacked it out of his hand.

"You know what? Fine. I'll just riffle through some cultural encyclopedias or something. It's not like I'm already having a bad time. Now I'm seeing shit and I have stupid homework about it." Jack threw his arms up in exasperation and turned away.

THE NOTEBOOK

They spent about a week on the notebook. August wasn't an amazing artist, but really, that wasn't the point. The point was to be able to reference things Jack saw. So he drew everything haphazardly in colored pencil. It was frightening how broad a selection of objects and people were present in Jack's world but missing from August's.

There were six people who appeared regularly. Two of the six tried to talk to Jack: a girl and some small child. The other four people just came and went randomly. There were also various animals—half of which were completely unidentifiable and very difficult to describe.

But what Jack liked the most, and what August found most interesting, were the objects. All of them were kind of old-looking, according to Jack, and he kept finding similar versions of them in the school encyclopedia, which really freaked out August.

Jack had begun collecting odds and ends from his world in the corner of his room. He put tape around the area so August wouldn't stumble over the pile or break anything.

It didn't seem like August could interact with anything, but they didn't want to test that theory just yet.

What is this?

like this?

FIND THIS

MORE
LIKE
THIS

Stop Making
Those!

I KNOW
gross

LUNCH

"I didn't know you had a tattoo." Gordie flicked at the back of his neck annoyingly. "Where'd you get it?"

"Jack did it a couple months ago." August flipped up his collar so it was out of sight.

"You let someone who isn't a licensed professional stab you multiple times instead of just going to the next town over and getting it done by someone who actually knows what they're doing?" Alex looked horrified.

August shrugged. He could feel his ears getting hot.

"Did you guys do buddy tattoos? Does he have one, too?" Gordie pried, pulling at August's collar. He smacked her hand away and scowled.

"I just wanted it and Jack was there so he did it for me. It's not a big deal."

"It's just seems kind of unsanitary. *And* reckless," Alex said, pointing her plastic spork at August accusatorily.

"Uncharacteristically reckless." Gordie narrowed her eyes suspiciously.

"He's a drug dealer, Gordie. I'm sure that recklessness is a part of the job description. And stop bothering him before he gets so red his face bursts into flames."

They laughed as August silently thanked all the gods listening for Alex.

"Do you think Jack would do me one, too?" Gordie asked. "I tried to get one done at a shop, but I'm not eighteen yet so they kicked me out . . ."

August thought about Gordie lying under Jack. Imagined her replicating that tense silence that sometimes made his heart race if he thought about it for too long. He didn't like it.

"No. He wouldn't."

GLASS SHOES

Carrie-Anne had dragged Jack away to go shopping for matching Homecoming crap, so August found himself alone on a Saturday. He took the bus out to the end of the city to visit Rina alone. She looked surprised when she opened the door, but let him in anyway.

"Are you busy?"

"No," she said, tying her hair up in a sloppy bun on the top of her head. "I was just doing some reading."

"What kind?" August took off his shoes, placed them neatly by the door, and sprawled across her couch.

"Fairy tales."

August grinned. "You still read fairy tales?"

"Every part of the human condition is packaged neatly in fairy tales. Every bit of culture that makes us who we are." She tutted at him. "When I was a girl, such things were regarded with respect."

"I've always had trouble with that," he replied dryly.

Rina scoffed and settled down on the floor. "I know. But one day you'll learn it. All virtues not granted at birth are taught to you by life, one way or another. My mother told me that."

"Your mother sounds wonderful," August said, closing his eyes.

"She was."

THE KINGDOM

Jack lay on his back on Rina's carpet. She had gone to work hours ago, but she didn't mind if they stayed. Jack brushed his hand lazily against the fibers like he was stroking the edges of a current. August smoked next to him and stared out the window. He flicked his lighter on and off.

"Can you describe it to me?" August said suddenly. "I want to hear all of it. I want to hear what I look like. What I'm wearing."

Jack closed his eyes. "Sometimes it changes. At first, you were wearing a mask. This big, feathered thing made of bone and gold with a long, pointed nose like a hawk. It was scary at first, but I got used to it. After the time that we fought at the river, you don't wear it anymore—I just see you. Sometimes you're in regular clothes and sometimes, like now, you're wearing leather armor and boots. It suits you."

August ran a hand down his sweater.

"Your hair is wilder, too. Not plastered down and combed like you like it." Jack reached out and August handed him his cigarette. He blew the smoke up.

"Back near town there are silver birds that are as bold as pigeons. They get really close to us sometimes. There are things like cows, but they have an extra set of horns and their legs are too long. Everyone is very tall. The houses in the city are made of sticks and mud and reinforced with wood and gold. The people here don't seem to think gold is rare, because it's all over everything. Right now we're not by all the buildings, though. We're on a hill near a burned and rotting forest. It's very dark and I can barely see either sun through the gloom or fog or whatever." Jack took another drag and handed the cigarette back with a grimace. "It's terrifying."

"I'm sorry."

"It's not your fault."

August put out his cigarette. "What's it like when you close your eyes?" he asked.

Jack just sighed and ignored him.

THE WICKER KING

Jack shoved a crumpled piece of paper in his hands as he passed him in the hall. August uncrumpled it in his next class and spread it out neatly across the desk. He read the message that was penned in Jack's blocky slapdash handwriting:

We need to talk. I saw this written on a wall. You know where . . . anyway, I wrote it down quickly because I thought it might help:

The rob in the roan
The biggleby's sown,
And grown!
For who can call its own?

For fee be we who wiggle must
Through doom and dust
But vain in trust
And Rapturous Blue, most fiery blust
Stands firm in the Hall that bends for us all.
But.

When the Cloven King rises will and whey
The Bigsbanes scatter and the Worrig pray

And Gorgon swees the morth and may
For fain will comest, direst day!

The blowings' blowing and the coldings' colding
And the biggleby's scritch-scratch wanes and dies
And the gallumps burst with rules and lies
Because the Fortentook draws ever nigh!
Will the Bigsbanes weep and the Gorgon cry,
"The Wicker King comes, for you nor I?"

The Wicker King. August shivered from the back of his neck down to his toes. Then he shoved the paper in the deepest part of his backpack and tried not to think about it.

ANALYSIS

"Jack, that is gibberish."

"You're telling me this like it's news."

August stared at Jack, then stared at the paper, then looked back up at Jack.

"Stop looking at me like that. It totally makes sense if you look at it long enough. Kind of like analyzing a poem for English. Like the bigglebys have to be some kind of crop or, like, a term for general agricultural prosperity? I don't know. The only thing I'm sure of is that the Cloven King is bad. People are relying on the Wicker King, and whatever he used to protect them in the hall of whatever is gone and needs to be returned or shit will hit the fan. Are you up for it?"

"Up for what? What can we even do?" August said, slumping over his desk.

"Personally, I think we should save them. It sounded pretty dire. And just because they're not a part of this world doesn't mean they're worth less than we are. That is prejudice." Jack sniffed dramatically. "Anyway, you're a lot better than me at analyzing poetry, so can you just look at this for me and figure out what we're supposed to do?"

"Jack. This won't fix the problem," August said darkly.

They both knew what problem he was referring to.

"I know," Jack said. "But please."

MONKEY WRENCH

August stashed the poem in his bag for a week. He didn't like looking at it.

Peter and Roger were giving him knowing gazes all the time and, quite frankly, it was beginning to get on his nerves.

Homecoming was in two days.

Two of the drug runners he worked with had gotten caught, so Daliah pushed their workload onto him and it was making him nervous. He liked the extra money, but not enough to risk serious jail time.

Jack's parents hadn't been home in ages and that made him anxious, too. Jack seemed to be all right with it. But it was hard not to be concerned when your best friend went home every day to darkness and food from a can.

His back had been hurting lately, too. It was a dull, persistent ache along his shoulders and up his neck. Probably stress. What else would it fucking be?

FRIDAY,
UNDER THE BLEACHERS

"Hey, boy, hey."

August cracked open an eye and gazed up.

"Come get me at eight tonight?"

He closed his eyes again.

"You didn't forget that tonight's the dance, did you?" Gordie huffed.

"I didn't forget," August said tiredly. "I got a suit ready and everything."

Gordie bent down lower to get a closer look at him. "You look unusually ragged. Like exhausted and shit."

August just gave her the finger and closed his eyes. "I'm doing my best, kid. Take it or leave it."

Gordie laughed and sprinkled some grass over his face. "Yeah, yeah, yeah. Get some sleep, babe. And don't forget: pick me up at eight."

FRENCH CUT SILK

"Come here," August said. "I can't believe no one taught you how to do this."

"Well, you know. My dad's not around a lot . . . so . . ."

Jack tilted his head back. August laughed nervously as he tied his friend's bow tie.

It was soft. The moment was *soft*.

"Why aren't you getting dressed at Carrie-Anne's? You know she likes that stuff. You know? Matching and crap," August said, pulling the fabric gently.

"So do you, you dick," Jack shot back. "But yeah . . . I don't think she'll give me any time to myself at Homecoming, so . . . I just . . ."

Jack shrugged helplessly. He couldn't finish. He never did.

August just sighed and tugged the knot tight.

HOMECOMING

His mother had taught him to waltz. She had been in pageants. A real glamour girl with her tiara on straight and a smile like a thousand diamonds. Hand cupped *just so* to wave with grace to the cheering crowd. She came from money; they thought learning those sort of things was important.

The only waving she did now was at him sometimes when he went to school, and the only thing cheering was the television in the basement. But she hadn't always been that way.

So August knew where to put his hands and he knew where to place his feet. He knew to rub the back of Gordie's neck with his thumb to make her shiver. She pressed against him tightly.

Across the room, Jack watched.

He was with Carrie-Anne of course. She had shoved herself into a bright pink monstrosity and piled her hair up high on her head in some kind of curl nest. They were doing the traditional sway-from-side-to-side dance that pretty much everyone else was doing. Jack smirked at August over Carrie-Anne's shoulder.

August rolled his eyes and decided to ignore him. He leaned his forehead against Gordie's neck. She smelled sweet, like incense and hair spray.

"Do you want to go back to mine? My parents won't be back till . . ."

"Yes. Fucking yes," he said.

BANG BANG

They tumbled to the carpet and Gordie slammed his head against the door. It was like being pillaged. He liked the roughness. He didn't care where it came from.

When she tore his tie off and dug her hands into his pants, he practically collapsed. He was all shaking hands and breathy gasps to her sharp claws and shouted expletives.

Gordie rode him like he wasn't made of skin and bone.

August smoothed her hair out of her face tenderly, but she batted his hand away. He rubbed his thumbs into her hips, so she bit his neck. He scratched his fingers against the shaved part of her head and she made a pretty, pretty noise. He leaned his head back and closed his eyes as she ate him alive.

When she pulled him back roughly by his hair, August gasped, arching off the floor.

She wasn't allowed to do that. No one did that except *him*. He reached up a hand to pull her arm off him, but she swiveled her hips and it was too late.

He fell. Groaning. Thinking of chapped lips, strong arms, and freckles.

Peter snatched the poem from August's hand and glanced at it quickly. "This is gibberish," he said. Roger peered over his brother's shoulder with interest.

"No. It's not," August insisted. "I need you to analyze it so I can figure out what Jack and I have to do."

"What you *have* to do is get him to a psychologist," Peter said dryly.

"But—!" Roger chimed in before August could respond to the threat. "We'll take a look at it for you. So far, it looks like some kind of quest."

August nodded solemnly. A quest. He could do that. At least it wasn't telling him they had to kill people.

"We'll get back to you tomorrow. You can go." Peter waved him away.

August scowled at Peter's rudeness, but picked up his backpack off the grass and left the twins alone under the bleachers.

FIRST RECEIVER FALCON

August met him in front of the locker room right after the game. Jack stumbled in with the rest of the team. He took off his scrum cap and wiped the sweat and dirt from his face.

"We are in the very middle of the country," he panted, with no preamble whatsoever. "Where the government is located. We move through their world like they move through my field of vision. Which means most people can't see you, but they know you're there. Also, the layers concept we've been discussing was actually more spot-on than we originally thought. I'm pretty sure places here actually coincide directly with places in the capital city."

"When did you figure this out?"

Jack smirked. "Well, I'm reasonably certain the pitch out there is a marketplace. It was really fucking distracting with all the stalls and people popping up and phasing out. One of the goalposts was a fountain for at least half the game." Jack shook his head.

"Wow. I don't even know what to say . . ." August was horrified. He'd had no idea it was that bad already. "Well, I gave the poem to the twins. They're helping us. Maybe they can figure out—"

"What?! Why?"

August rolled his eyes. "I'll explain later. Get dressed and meet me at the toy factory around six o'clock. Your teammates are starting to stare."

SICK TRICK

Jack pulled into the toy factory employee parking lot and turned off his engine. "Why did you give the poem to the twins?" Jack demanded through the window. He didn't sound happy.

August slid into the passenger's seat. "Peter noticed something going on with you months ago and he came to me about it. Roger found out by default. Their mom is a *psychologist*. I couldn't do anything about it. They figured it out, so now they're involved. They promised not to tell anyone if we don't hurt anyone or don't get hurt ourselves . . ." August trailed off as Jack narrowed his eyes.

"What? *I can't do anything about it now*," August continued. "We're deadlocked with them right now. Our actions dictate their response. The twins are methodical like that. . . . Though, your conjecture is a good advancement for us. Honestly, the quicker we fix this, the better."

"Fix this?" Jack asked, his hands gripping the steering wheel tightly. "Is that why I'm supposed to meet you here"

"We have to test the limits of your sight and make a map so we can navigate the city in relation to our town. I figured here would be as good a starting place as any . . ."

Jack was silent awhile, staring through the windshield. "I'm going to do this by myself. I don't need you for this anymore," he said quietly.

"No! You can't just—we've gotten so far already. Don't cut me out, Jack. *Please*."

"Get out of my car."

"No!"

"Get the fuck out of my car!" Jack shouted.

August slammed the door hard behind him. He didn't look back as Jack tore out of the parking lot and sped off into the night.

COMMUNION

August's legs pulled him from the town to the heart of the woods. It was over a mile away. The wind whipped against his face, numbing his cheeks and stinging his eyes. He gathered branches, ripping them from trees and pulling them from the forest floor, ignoring the tug and scrape of the bark on his hands. He worked mindlessly, *robotically*. Bending and standing and dropping and bending and standing and dropping.

When the brush reached the swell of his thighs, he set it ablaze. The flames were as tall as he was.

August collapsed against a tree and slid to the ground, his feet swollen in his shoes, palms bleeding and dirty. He lay there like a dead thing. Eyes wide and glassy, staring into the flames.

It burned deep into the night.

August waited until the last ember sank into black. Then he climbed slowly to his feet, knelt by the charred remains, and sank his fingers into the ash.

RAW

This "world" wasn't real. But it was real for Jack, so that made it real for him. This was a decision. August was *choosing* this. He wasn't Alice falling unaware down the rabbit hole—that was Jack.

August?

He'd seen Jack fall and sprinted toward the pit; August had leaped off the edge and dove headlong into the darkness behind him. He would pull them both out of the deep with his bare hands.

It was the debt. The river. It was his religion now.

And such a thing was worth more than the mountains and the seas.

REMUS

He walked back to town and straight to Jack's house. To his surprise, Jack's mom opened the door when he knocked. She hadn't been home in weeks. He frowned at her with undisguised disapproval.

"Hi, August. May I help you?"

"I need to see Jack."

Jack's mom looked concerned. "I don't know if you should. He's not feeling very well."

"Even more reason that I should see him. I'm the only one who ever does anything about it anyway," August said meanly.

He pushed past her and headed up the stairs. August opened Jack's door without knocking and shut it behind him. Jack was crouched in the corner in the dark, his head buried in his arms. August strode fast to him and dropped to his knees. He lifted Jack's face and gripped it tight in his hands.

"I was just scared," Jack whispered.

"I know." He wiped a tear from Jack's cheek, smearing his face with ash.

"Don't leave me."

August shut his eyes. "I *won't*."

CULTURAL STUDIES

Rina took off her apron and scooted into the booth with them. Jack pushed the poem across the table to her, then leaned back in his chair as she read. She'd taken her hair down out of the tight bun she always wore for work. By the time she got to the bottom of the page, she was frowning.

"What does it mean?" August demanded.

"I only took half a semester of folklore at the community college, so—"

"You're the best we've got right now," August interrupted. "Anything you can give us would be good."

Rina tapped a bobby pin on the paper and looked thoughtful. "So, the Wicker King is from a game you used to play when you were kids, right?" They both nodded. "What were the rules?"

"It was an imagination game. More of a power play than anything else, I'm beginning to realize," Jack said dryly. "It was a classic adventure story. Pretend hunting, pretend feasts, pretend sword fighting with sticks."

Rina squinted. "If I were to compare this poem to others I've seen, it's kind of like a really simple rhymeless lai. Or a prophecy of some kind. If you scrap the nonsense words and only focus on the words in English, it's a pretty simple narrative."

She slid the plate holding the remainder of August's apple pie to her side of the table and took a quick bite.

"Basically, there is an object, the so-called Rapturous Blue, that has been taken from its home. And that's not a good thing because without it, everyone and everything in the story is going to die. Because of some other evil Cloven King. The Wicker King—that's you," she said to Jack, "has to go and find the Rapturous Blue and bring it back so whatever the Fortentook is doesn't happen. So I'm assuming that whatever Jack is seeing is following that basic narrative."

"That doesn't . . . sound . . . good," Jack said.

August leaned forward and put his elbows on the table. His heart was racing. "What do you suggest we do?"

Rina shrugged. "Personally, I'd take him to the hospital."

"We're not doing that," Jack said quickly.

"Why?" Rina frowned.

"Because I said so. We're going to fulfill the prophecy."

"Are you fucking crazy?" August spat.

"Why are you so afraid of a little adventure? Nothing cool ever happens in this stupid town." Jack grinned mirthlessly. "Besides, we're already playing one game. Why not add another? Do you think you can't handle it?"

"What game? The one from when you were kids?" Rina asked. She looked suspicious.

"No, not really," Jack said vaguely. "We're too old for that one. This one is different."

August drummed his fingers on the table. He couldn't even begin to think of how to explain what had happened at the river earlier that year. Much less illustrate the concept of "games" and what they had grown to mean. He thought about Jack's fingers at the back of his neck and tasted a bit of shame. "Quit baiting her, Jack. Rina, it's nothing. I'll tell you later," August lied.

BESTIARY: BEASTIARY

"It was a bright place," Jack said. Everything was hyperrealistic and detailed. The only way he knew something was real sometimes was if it was unspeakably drab. "But it's almost a closed circuit now."

Before, he'd mostly seen people in drab, but these days it was all reds and yellows and greens. The clothes were different, rustic. They were running out of time.

"If things get too far, like I know they will, write down everything I say and describe. Everything that happens. Everything," Jack said.

Of course August would. Of course he *did*. It was too good a story for him not to.

August purchased ten notebooks and thirty pens. Slotted a pen into each notebook and bound the rest with a rubber band. Now he never left the house without a pen and notebook.

ORDINARY

The woods were still the woods in Jack's world. Most areas without urban alteration were basically the same. The older something was, the more likely it was to remain exactly as Jack had remembered it from before; he couldn't tell the difference.

The oldest thing in town was the river. It flowed over nearly the exact same path as the river in the other world, and August figured it was comforting to Jack because of the regularity with which he demanded to go there these days.

Based on what he'd described, wherever Jack was, was somewhere in the East around the heyday of the Silk Road, maybe earlier. At least that was about the level of technological advancement that there was to deal with. Jack had taken objects from this other world and stashed them in the corner of his room. He described them in detail; some had parallel histories here. For a while, August suspected that it wasn't so much *where* Jack was but *when* Jack was.

"So what about the Rapturous Blue?" August asked, pulling his pen out of the spirals of the notebook. "What is it?"

Jack closed his eyes. "It's like . . . it's like a star. Or like a god made of . . . rock? It's difficult to describe . . . but it's small enough to hold in your hand. And so bright that you can barely stand to look at it. Like . . . a very small star? I don't know. I don't have all the answers, August. It's a big, shiny magical star battery thing and everyone is dying now that it's gone. It's causing their version of the apocalypse, I think."

"Annnd . . . how are we going to find it?"

"I don't know, but I'll find it. I have to."

NULL HYPOTHESIS

Jack held Rina's hand as he pulled her up the hill.

They wanted to show Rina a bit more of what Jack was seeing so they could test the validity of their theory. They agreed that Rina was enough of an impartial observer that her opinion would have more impact than August's. Jack had brushed his knuckles across August's chin in a parody of a blow and said, "I've gotta know that you're not just telling me what I want to hear."

August's eyes were locked on Jack's hand grasping Rina's. It made his stomach feel so . . .

"You can see the whole town from up here," Jack said.

The hill put them just high enough that they could see the lights of the buildings fading into the dark beyond the town.

"What do you see?" Rina asked.

"Everything. There are stone buildings in the middle of the town that turn into wood ones, then into mud ones the farther from the center you go. Over by where the toy factory should be there is a larger building made of white stone. It's like a church or a town hall or something. There are a couple of fields where animals are grazing . . ."

"At night?" Rina scrunched up her nose.

"They can see in the dark or they're being guided," Jack finished.

From their hilltop, they could see a few people walking their dogs at the dog park below.

August came shoulder to shoulder with Rina and nudged her gently. She looked sad.

"It's okay," August whispered.

Jack turned suddenly to look at them.

"The birds like you," he said to Rina, dropping her hand. He reached forward and cupped some air near her shoulder. "They're fluttering near."

He shifted his dark eyes to August, and August's heart thudded like the monstrous march of time. Jack tilted his head to the side and stared into the depths of him.

"Everywhere you go, everything is wilder around you. You brought the birds, but they're staying for her . . . I think. It's a good omen."

He offered a smile, then looked back out at the town.

"The buildings fade to trees, the trees fade to bramble, the bramble fades to dust, and beyond is the land of forgotten kings. The Wastes. Where nothing lives, nothing grows, and nothing dies."

"Nothing dies?" Rina asked, huddling closer to Jack.

He slipped his hand back into hers. "Nothing dies. At least that's what they write on the walls. They write all sorts of things on the walls of stone buildings—prayers, jokes, news. But mostly warnings. They say that beyond the wild woods, which is the area closest to the town, there are large, rabid beasts and swarms of gore crows. Those are like dead birds that eat living flesh."

Jack shivered.

"They say that if your milkbeasts get lost in the wild woods, you should just leave them there. That it is less costly than going out to find them and paying with your life."

"How do you live like this?" Rina whispered.

Jack shrugged.

"Where we are, it is light." The wind blew hard from the east and the trees rustled their branches.

"From where I'm standing . . . it is warm enough."

FROST

Winter break was coming up.

Daliah was *really* riding his ass about deliveries. More and more kids were getting pinched, and she had more supply than people who could hawk it. Honestly, August wanted to just quit, but his mom's disability benefits had been cut and he really couldn't afford to.

Along with that looming over his head, his notebooks were getting pretty full and it was becoming clearer than ever that Jack's condition was getting worse and worse every day. It was good to feel like they were doing something proactive about it, though. They'd nearly mapped out the entire town and a bit of the woods.

It was also good to have some other people around who knew what was going on. The twins had been remarkably helpful when August wasn't there to watch Jack at all times, even though Jack still deeply resented their involvement. Peter was still an asshole about it, but at least they hadn't told anyone yet.

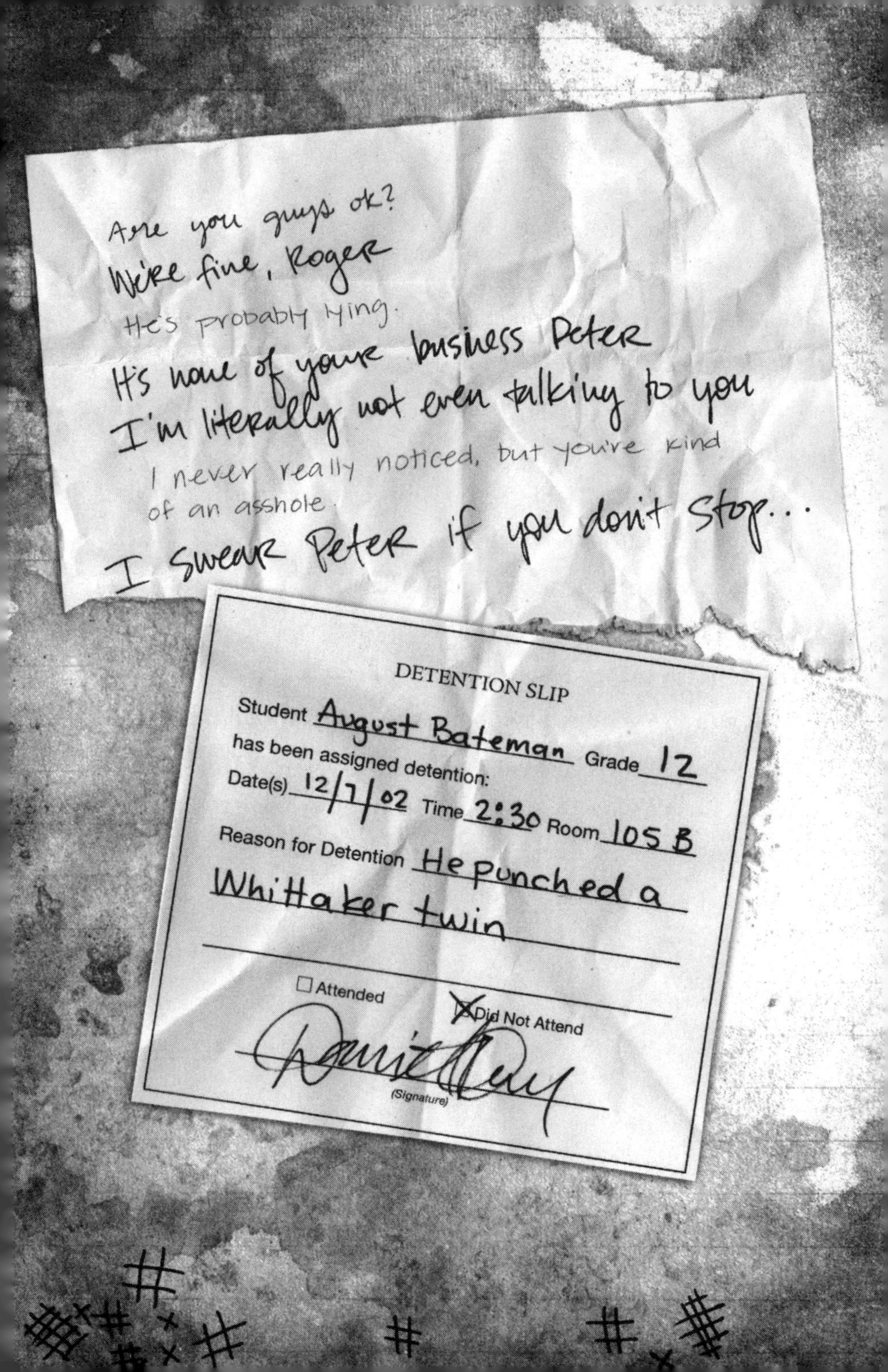
Are you guys ok?
We're fine, Roger
He's probably lying.
It's none of your business Peter
I'm literally not even talking to you
I never really noticed, but you're kind of an asshole.
I swear Peter if you don't stop...

DETENTION SLIP
Student August Bateman
has been assigned detention: Grade 12
Date(s) 12/7/02 Time 2:30 Room 105 B
Reason for Detention He punched a Whittaker twin

☐ Attended
☒ Did Not Attend

(Signature)

"We need to find a way for you to interact with my world so you can put the Rapturous Blue on its stand and have it actually work. The Cloven King rides closer every day and the city is decaying all around me. I can't do it by myself."

"Yeah. I know." August kicked at a pebble as they trudged to the toy factory. "Do you have any ideas?"

Jack grimaced sheepishly. "I have a couple, but none of them are good."

August pulled out a loose panel of glass and they scrambled inside the factory. Jack climbed down from the windowsill and offered August a hand. August ignored it and leaped down instead, landing hard and rolling to his feet. Jack watched appreciatively.

"You're getting good at that."

August shrugged off the compliment. "Where is the stand?"

"Is there anything in here that's in the middle of the room? I can remember there being like some kind of—"

"The only thing in the middle of the room is one of those water coolers that people have at offices that give cold and hot water," August interrupted.

Jack lit up. "Really? Oh sweet! I'm pretty sure the Rapturous Blue goes in the area where you'd put a cup. I see it like a really decorative metal tower thing with a square slot in the middle.

Also, for your information, we're in the city's town hall–slash–church-museum thing. It's really fancy in here."

"Even if we find the Rapturous Blue, we can't put it in now because . . . ?"

"It won't work, August. We've gone over this," Jack said, sounding annoyed. "There needs to be, like, some conduit that allows you to reach through this world into mine. Otherwise, it would be like putting a dead battery in a flashlight and expecting it to turn on."

August scoffed in exasperation. "Okay. So, what we're looking for is something that would give enough of a charge? All right. At least that's an achievable goal . . ." He walked around the room looking at all the machinery. He casually picked up a plastic doll head off the floor and tossed it in the air, catching it deftly in his hand.

"Can . . . we leave?" Jack asked, sounding suddenly cagey.

"Why? We just got here."

Jack didn't respond. He just fidgeted a bit.

August didn't even sigh. He walked over to the window, climbed the wall, and pulled out the glass. "Woods, river, or field?"

"Field. I want to run."

They ran until it hurt to pull the cold air through their teeth. The snow had melted, and the grass was frozen and crunchy. They tumbled to the ground, panting hard. Jack coughed, then winced, grasping the side of his head.

"You okay?"

"Yeah. It just hurt for a minute . . . but I'm fine."

August curled toward him, and Jack grabbed August's jacket, pulling him closer. He rested his forehead against August's.

"Do you want to know how I see you?" Jack's voice was roughened from the run. August nodded. "I see you the same. I don't think it will ever change. . . . It doesn't matter if you're wearing my colors or dressed like this. You're always just you."

"What does it mean?"

"I don't know. But I don't want that to go away." Jack swallowed. "If it does, I don't think it would be good."

"I'm not going anywhere," August insisted, curling his fingers into the grass.

"That's not what I meant."

INDIGO

Jack lay on the floor of Rina's apartment. He threaded his fingers through the dingy carpet. August sat next to him and quietly watched as Rina pulled her stockings up her legs and clipped them to her garter belt. She shimmied into her uniform and zipped it up the back.

His favorite thing was watching her put on her makeup. He liked the dark liquid she spread around her eyes to make them deeper. He didn't really know what everything else she used was, but the way she slathered it on was like an art. She was stunning in the dim yellow light.

Rina waited until the very last to put on her lipstick. It was like war paint, red and vivid, smeared across her mouth.

She smiled at August for effect.

He shivered.

Rina puttered around the apartment as she worked, washing dishes, picking up clothes, quickly eating a bowl of Shredded Wheat. It was startlingly domestic.

"We have to go on a trip," Jack said suddenly.

"Why?" August looked up at him from where he was lying on the carpet.

"To find the Rapturous Blue," Jack said, like it was the most obvious thing in the world.

"Where?" Rina asked.

"Not that far. We don't have to do it right now, if that's what you were wondering. I just need to go and dig it up."

"In our world or in yours? And how do you even know where it is?"

"Mine. And I just *know*. I can feel it," Jack replied flippantly. "It's kind of like when someone is staring at you and you're not looking back at them, but you just know that they're looking at you. I know what direction to head in to get close to it because I can feel it. It sounds dumb, but just go with it, okay?"

August took one more drag of his cigarette and looked at Jack suspiciously. "When was the last time you hung out with any of your other friends?" he asked.

Jack looked nervous. He picked at Rina's carpet awhile and

looked out the window. "I don't remember. I've been phasing them out slowly. I can't deal with it, you know? The pretending. It does my head in."

"It would do mine in, too, if I had to do what you do," Rina said, "You'd probably make a good actor if this ever gets fixed." She started heavily powdering over her makeup.

"Rina, could you do me next?" August joked, putting his cigarette out on a nearby plate.

"No, you tart, I'm busy. I have a reading in fifteen minutes."

"At that same shitty café?" He laughed.

Rina pushed him playfully and kissed them both good-bye before she left.

BOLT

August lit another cigarette in the gloom. He looked over at Jack, who was sitting very still. The curve of his head was round in the light through Rina's cracked, yellowed lampshade.

Sometimes they waited for her to get back from work or from reading poetry at the café. Just passing the time lying on the carpet or playing cards or watching crap TV on her tiny fifteen-inch box.

Jack picked at his jeans nervously, then went still again. He was like this marvelous creature. It was impossible not to scrutinize him if given the chance. Jack was like a deer now, poised as if about to run. August wondered what would happen if he touched him—just reached out and dragged his finger up the side of his neck . . .

Before he could even make real contact, Jack spun around lightning fast and gripped August's wrist hard. Grinding the bones in his fist. August made a sharp sound of hurt and pulled back.

He'd forgotten his place.

Jack loosened his grip and peered at him curiously. "Sometimes I don't understand you, August. You're very bold."

August swallowed, but didn't look away.

THE BEGINNING

"So. The trip. When is that happening?"

"I'm thinking we could go out during winter break. Of course we'll be back by Christmas, but I think we need at least a day or two." Jack headed down August's street with his headlights on dim.

"What are we getting?"

"Something that I think will help us. I've been talking to her—"

"Rina?" August asked.

"Oh my God, yes, stop interrupting. Anyway, she explained things a bit more succinctly, and I have a pretty good idea of what we need to do now."

August looked tired. "And what is that?"

Instead of answering, Jack bit his lip and turned smoothly into August's driveway.

"I'm not going to like it, am I?"

"Probably not."

August sighed.

KEEP WARM

August went downstairs. He didn't do so very often because he didn't like it—the stale smell of old, decaying furniture, stifling muggy air, the tinny buzz of the Game Show Network. But she was down here and he needed her permission.

"August?"

"Hey, Mom . . ."

He couldn't remember when she had begun spending most of her time down here. It had been sometime when he was in middle school, after his dad left. August leaned down to kiss her on her blond head and ignored the scent of old sweat and medicine.

"I want to go on a trip with Jack this Saturday."

"When will you be back?" Her eyes never left the screen.

"Monday. Winter break is starting, so I don't have class."

"Oh. That's nice . . ." Someone was guessing how much a blender cost. August stood there for a couple of minutes, watching over her shoulder. Then he pulled the quilt up and tucked it around her.

"Did Dad send the check yet?" he asked. "It's getting cold out—the gas is getting more expensive." He put his hand on her forehead to check for fever, just in case. She nodded under his fingers but didn't look up at him.

The audience cheered. "Okay. I love you," August said.

She didn't hear him.

FOND

Jack drove up at 6:00 a.m. "We're going to Iowa," he said excitedly, letting himself into the kitchen.

"What?! That's two whole states away!"

"Yup." Jack rummaged in August's fridge, taking out a couple of bottles of water. "And that's where we're going. We're going to find the Rapturous Blue."

August didn't even try to argue. He just slung his travel bag over his shoulder, tucked a blanket under his arm, and followed Jack outside. "Where's your car?"

Jack happily patted the side of a truck that stood where Jack usually parked his car. "My grandpa is letting me borrow his pickup. Anyway, I was thinking we'd drive until like three, then stop somewhere and switch."

"I can't believe I'm doing this. Does this truck even have heat? I bet I'm paying for gas." August could hear himself whining, but he didn't care. "Why do we have to leave so early? I haven't had breakfast . . ." He swung into the passenger's seat and almost hit his face on the brown paper bag Jack was holding out toward him.

"I know you, man. Peanut butter and banana, wheat bread, no crusts. Go wild."

"Oh."

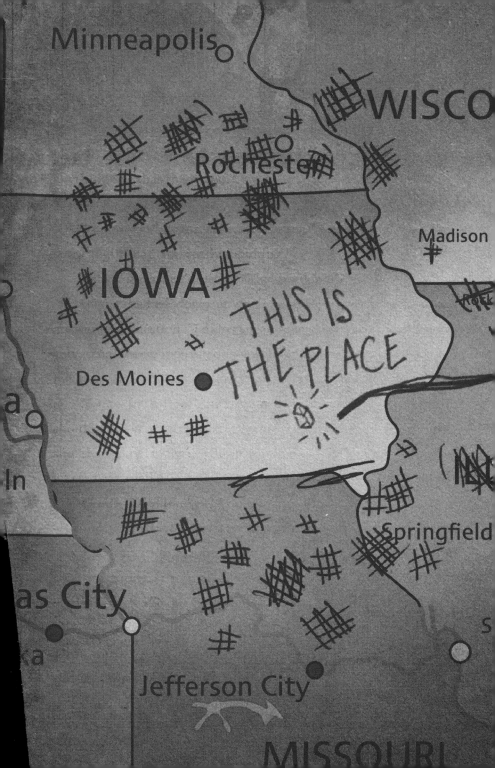

He didn't even bother to look at Jack as he snatched the bag petulantly. He knew the son of a bitch was grinning at him fondly or something. August began wolfing down his food and Jack put the truck in drive.

PROSPECT

Driving places with Jack felt safe, like riding with a parent. He was really good at it. Way better than August was. He'd learned early, when they were about fourteen. Sneaking Jack's father's car out of the garage at night to go cruise into the dark. . . .

Jack's grandpa's truck didn't have a radio, just rattling and the hum of the engine. Jack whistled quietly to himself while August chain-smoked and napped in the sun.

"Are you seeing anything now?" August asked curiously, breaking the silence.

"Always."

"Does it . . . you know . . . get in the way of driving?"

"You're asking me this after thirty miles?" Jack asked dryly. "I'm doing fine. We aren't dead yet."

That was not a comforting response. "Can I just drive the rest of the way?"

"Will you stop complaining if we stop at a Cracker Barrel?" Jack teased. "I know your complex relationship with that chain."

"Cracker Barrel is *great*. It is a restaurant and a toy store and a souvenir store all in one. We've been over this," August said curtly.

"Mmm." Jack hummed in lieu of a reply. He sounded way too satisfied for someone who was most definitely going to be turning left into that parking lot and paying for both of their lunches. "Don't worry so much. We'll be finished with this and be on our way back home soon."

HICKORY

Something suddenly occurred to August. "What ever happened to Carrie-Anne?"

Jack paused for a second, then continued sawing away at his steak and eggs. "We broke up after Homecoming. We got into a fight. She . . . thought I wasn't paying enough attention to her. I think she was starting to notice the—" Jack waved his hand around instead of describing what was happening with his mind. "Plus, she's not exactly great at keeping secrets, so I couldn't just tell her. I had to let her go."

August stopped eating and put down his fork. "You didn't even tell me . . ."

"Yeah, well." Jack looked tired and embarrassed.

"I'm sorry." August didn't know what to say. He hadn't even noticed. "Really. I mean, I hated her, but you really liked her . . ."

"It's okay," Jack mumbled. "We're too busy for that right now anyway. It's not important. Finish your food. We have to get back on the road."

DUSK

August drove until after the sun went down. Jack had fallen asleep almost as soon as they switched seats, after handing August a crumpled piece of paper with directions on it and curling up toward the window.

August felt young as he drove in the dark in the middle of nowhere—a place with no houses or tall buildings or people around. Just miles of road and grass and cars and the sound of Jack breathing gently in his sleep beside him. They were only seventeen. The world was so big and they were very small and there was no one around to stop terrible things from happening.

Suddenly he felt panicked. He wanted Jack awake right now. "Jack. *Jack!*"

Jack shifted sleepily, but eventually turned and glared at him. "What?"

August didn't know what to say; he hadn't thought that far.

"What?" Jack asked again, sounding annoyed. "Did you want to switch?"

"No. I just . . . got bored."

Jack looked at him skeptically.

"It's fine. It's nothing. Go back to sleep," August mumbled, embarrassed.

Jack sighed and reached over, gripping the back of August's neck firmly in his hand. The tension instantly bled from August's bones and he breathed out softly. "We'll stop in an hour."

MOTEL

There was not much sleeping that night.

They had both stared at the mottled, ratty hotel carpet for at least five whole minutes before collapsing together onto the single bed. Now sleeping with Jack was a hot, terrible ordeal with far too much elbow for August's tastes. The sheets were too scratchy and stank of the person who had lain in them before they did. But it was better than the floor.

It was hardly the first time they'd done this. They'd shared all the time when they were kids, Jack jabbing his sharp little knees and elbows into August's side in his sleep until August could take no more and shoved him unceremoniously off the bed and onto the floor. Then, to top it off, August would inevitably wake up with drool on the back of his neck, Jack having snuck back in while he was asleep . . .

"Get up."

August opened his eyes. He didn't remember drifting off, but apparently it was morning. Jack was dressed and packed. He looked like he wasn't interested in dealing with anyone's shit. August scrambled out of bed and started shoving his legs back into his jeans.

"We have to leave before three o'clock so we can be there by six thirty and be on our way as quickly as possible. I'm going to go grab some coffee. You should stretch a bit. We're going to be digging." Jack strode out of the room without a glance backward.

ROPE

"How much time do we have?"

"A half hour, maybe less. I know it's down there. I don't know how *far* or whatever, but I'm sure I'll be able to find it pretty quick. The real task is not getting caught. This is shoot-first-ask-questions-later territory. And when I say pull me up, you pull me up as fast as you can."

"Pull you up?!" August spluttered. "You have like thirty pounds of muscle on me. Why can't I be the one who—"

"I'm not in the mood," Jack interrupted, glaring at him.

August slumped in his seat and sulked. This was the worst road trip ever. When Jack reached toward him, August jerked away. "What?!"

"You have something on your face. Let me get it," Jack said, looking away from the road for a moment.

August frowned warily but sat still while Jack rubbed his face with the ball of his thumb. "Christ, you're such a child," Jack muttered.

August didn't dignify that with a response.

DEPTH

They wound up not having to dig at all. It was on a farmer's property in a well.

An ordinary well.

"Try not to breathe what's down there," August warned just before Jack climbed in without a word. He watched as Jack sank into the gloom. August would later say that this took less than a moment.

When he pulled Jack up, the rope heavy in his hands, he looked to see what Jack gripped tightly between his blackened fingers, wet with dirt. The token worth a hundred miles. The Rapturous Blue.

It was a *rock*.

Gray.

Plain.

Nothing.

RAPTUROUS BLUE

Jack let him hold it as he drove them back home. "Try not to look directly at it. It's too bright," he'd said as he gingerly handed over the rock, which he'd wrapped in his scarf.

August said nothing. He just took the rock and held it close. He didn't unwrap it; he didn't try to look at it. He just held it and tried not to cry. How did Jack even know where to go? Did it even matter?

He thought about Roger's phone number scrawled messily on a scrap of paper shoved into his desk drawer.

He thought about the look on Jack's face when he'd pushed him out of his car and said he didn't need him anymore.

He thought about just going home and sleeping forever.

It began to snow. It was almost Christmas.

CHROME

The drive passed quickly in silence. When they got back into town, Jack pulled into August's driveway and shut off the truck. August handed over the Rapturous Blue and Jack placed it gently in his lap.

"Thanks for, you know . . . coming with. I know you didn't have to."

August shrugged. They sat silently in the dark.

"Jack . . . I . . . ," he started to say. But Jack wouldn't look at him. "Are your parents going to be home for Christmas?" he asked. It wasn't what he'd planned to say.

"Yeah. My dad called when you were sleeping and said he planned to come home. He even said he's bringing a tree!" Jack sounded happy now.

Good.

"Okay," August said as he unlocked the door and stepped out. "Get some sleep. Tomorrow, we're going out into the field."

He didn't hear Jack drive away until he'd closed his house's door safely behind him.

Est. 1918

Monday, December 23r

Farmer Discovers Bismuth Deposit Beneath Old Well

Green holds bismuth crystal in hand

By Lynette Reeves

Local farmer Sherman Green, 54, recently discovered a large bismuth deposit on his property after a break-in. Green had been following the trail of a couple of trespassers that led to an abandoned well on his barley farm. The trespassers had left behind a couple of ropes, which Green said piqued his interest. "It was probably just a couple of stupid kids," Green said. "I had no idea why they'd come onto my land in the first place. They didn't steal anything... But that got me curious." Green decided to dig in the well and discovered a vein of bismuth deep beneath the surface. "I was so surprised. I didn't know exactly what it was that I'd found," said Green. "But it was beautiful, just beautiful. It was like fool's gold, but blue and rainbow all over."

Bismuth is a brittle metal commonly used in pharmaceuticals and cosmetics. The estimate on how much the vein is worth is somewhere around $700,000. As for the trespassers, Green says he's not interested in pressing charges. "You don't find something like that every day."

Is The Int Changing We do Bu

by Barry Stacks

Ten years ago, th
know it hit scre
when Explorer a
emerged as the l
Internet users. C
changed since th
several minutes t
page. Today, URL
as phone numbe
nesses.

During the las
been to the top o
world—during th
of the late 1990s
again, when it all
years later. But w
the good: The We
the business worl
small-business ov
examples of how
nologies can be a
best friend.

Because it cha
communicate in
Phoenix-based PI
http://www.pmp
vides test materia
agers studying fo
tification exams.
find prep courses,
study tools on the
ploys 11 people. B
site's founder, sta
PMP Tools by po

THE FIELD

As soon as they pulled up next to the field, August flew from the car and hit the ground running. The weeds and grass whacked at his jeans as he tore through the growth. He was glad that it hadn't snowed here. He could hear Jack behind him. Coming up swiftly.

This wasn't a race.

August sped toward the middle of the field, breathing the cold air quick, and Jack laughed. They thundered across, sneakers slipping in the dew, hearts pumping, throats heaving.

Caught. He could feel it. He was caught.

His lungs were crushed beneath long arms as they tumbled to the ground. Rolling rough, through green and gravel, biting and scratching like things that had claws and fangs instead of teeth and nails. August was pushed and pulled and rubbed in the ice-cold dirt, but he gave as good as he got.

"Call me 'sire.' Honor your king."

August just laughed. Jack slammed him down hard with a strong hand on his back.

Oh. So it was like that.

He resisted for longer than a moment. But it was just resistance. Not rebellion. "You're crushing me, *sire*," August said with as much sass as he could manage. He panted loud and hot into the grit.

Jack's gray eyes look light blue in the light. He let out a single breath that sounded like a smile.

POINSETTIA

His mom was *upstairs* and she was beautiful in red. Her hair was swept off her shoulders and she had earrings in her ears. She was even humming as she made Christmas dinner. August clung to her and kissed her cheek.

"Where's Jack?" she asked, stirring cheese into the macaroni.

"His dad is coming home."

"Are you sure? Call him before dinner starts." She ran her fingers through his hair, then wrinkled her nose. It had been weeks since his last haircut. August rolled his eyes—of all things she'd notice, it would be that. But to his surprise, she just shrugged and patted him on the cheek. "You never know. Make sure to call."

He hummed his assent and went to go phone Jack in the hallway. Jack's cell phone rang until August was certain it would go to voice mail. But it didn't.

"Did he come?" August asked.

Jack sobbed.

August put his shoes and coat on and went out into the cold.

GIFT

Jack lay on the floor next to August's bed on top of an unzipped sleeping bag. He'd wrapped the comforter and sheets that August's mom had especially reserved for him into a circular sort of nest and curled up in the middle of it.

She had even gotten Jack presents again this year, as if she'd expected him to come to Christmas all along. Even though they were struggling to get by and Jack could afford to pay for their entire Christmas dinner with the pocket money his parents left for him.

August peeked over the side of his bed and looked into the pile of covers. "Are you still awake?"

Jack didn't respond. He wasn't asleep, August knew that for certain. Jack snored like an engine full of glass and this was not that sound. This quiet, angry breathing was the sound of August being ignored.

August sighed. "If I ever see your father again, I'm going punch him in the face," he promised.

"I'll hold you to it."

JANUARY

August sucked the cold winter air through his teeth, then put out his cigarette on the side of the building. He spit on the ground quick and looked up to find Roger and Peter standing there watching him.

"You look haggard," Peter said bluntly. Roger pinched his brother and gave August an apologetic grimace.

"Well, it's nice to see the two of you haven't changed much over break." August shifted his bag over his shoulder and started walking toward their school's front door. They followed him.

"Gordie was looking for you," Roger said quietly.

They talked well enough when the three of them were alone, but he could already see Roger shutting that down in public—with Peter following his lead, as if in sympathy.

"We have to go now. But good luck," Roger murmured.

"Try not to fuck up things while we're gone." Peter sniffed as they walked past.

Yeah, whatever.

FINE FIERCE FIFTH

Gordie found him between fourth and fifth periods. "Missed you," she said, pushing him into the unused teachers' bathroom on the third floor.

He took her shirt off in a flurry, the two of them scrambling into a stall near the back. She sucked him off like they did this every day, then rode his fingers. Gordie laughed and said that his hair tickled her face as he kissed her neck. She squirmed in his arms with delight when they had finished, and called him pretty.

"Yeah, yeah, yeah," he said with a smile. "Get to class, you delinquent."

August watched her go, then wiped his hand on his jeans.

RUCK AND MAUL

"Where you been, man?"

"Nowhere. I've just been working through some stuff." August heard them before he saw them. Jack's friends had him backed against the lockers. "Are you joining cross-country with us during the off-season?"

"No. I can't. I'm busy."

"But Coach needs you, man! We've gotta stay in shape between seasons."

Jack looked up sharply and spotted August before August could duck back around the corner. Jack looked directly at him and said: "I'm not going to be there next season. So I don't need to join cross-country *this* season. I have to go." Then he pushed his way through his ex-teammates and walked down the hall.

"What do you mean, you're not playing next season?!" August asked as Jack passed.

"I don't want to talk about it. Let's *go*."

OCIMUM BASILICUM

August decided to go over to Jack's after school to cook him some food. He didn't know how to make much—just basic things like chili and grilled cheese and stuff. But Jack needed a home-cooked meal. Jack's parents hadn't been home in *weeks*. Hadn't been home since before Christmas. Their mail was so piled up under the mail slot, August briefly considered just shoving it all into a garbage bag and throwing it in their bedroom. It made him angry.

So here he was, trying his best to make a lasagna from instructions on the box.

Jack walked into the kitchen, leaned against the doorframe, and watched him quietly. August tossed a glance at him over his shoulder, but neither of them said anything. He felt Jack watching as he laid the noodles in a dish and poured sauce over them, then laid more down and spread the shredded cheese, arranging everything until he was satisfied. Then he slid the dish into the oven.

"I wish you could live here with me." It was almost a whisper.

August washed his hands in the sink and dried them roughly with a dish towel. "I can't. You know I can't. My mom, she—"

"I *know*. It was a *wish*, August." Jack finally moved from his spot near the door. He sat down at the kitchen table and held his head in his hands. "Why won't they come back?"

168

"I don't know," August said firmly. "You have to stop thinking about it. You'll destroy yourself. After dinner, we're going to the river."

August walked out of the kitchen so there was no room for argument.

VASSAL

Before they could reach the water, Jack slipped his hand into August's. He did it without asking. With confidence. Like it was meant to be there. August was pulled—complacently at first, then under wild protestation—right into the river. Pulled him in with their clothes still on and the water still rushing. So cold that it was but a mile and a minute from ice.

Jack pulled him in almost to his chest, then rested his head in the curve of August's neck. "What would you do for me?"

August shivered while he thought up an answer. "I don't know. Anything, probably."

"Do you really mean that?" It wasn't said with softness. It sounded like a threat.

Jack, misinterpreting August's silence as denial, dug his fingers into August's flesh. August gasped at the pain but didn't pull away.

"Come on. Let's get out of the water," August said gently. "Let's go home."

A lot of people were absent from lunch on Monday. This left him at the table with just Alex and Jack, who had emigrated quietly over to their friend group after quitting the team. Alex was studying for an AP exam and had spread her papers all over the place. August knocked the side of Alex's notebook away from her tray.

"Hey!"

August ignored her. "Do you know where Daliah is? I haven't seen her since we got back from break."

"Why should I tell you? You're rude." Alex sniffed as she pulled her papers toward her protectively.

"Tell him or I'll spill juice on your notes," Jack said threateningly, not looking up from his ravioli.

"Ugh. The both of you. I don't know why I even—" Alex shook her head. "Daliah was arrested on drug distribution charges. I doubt you'll see her again. They're really cracking down on that sort of . . . behavior. I would suggest you take the warning."

Jack gazed at August and raised an eyebrow in silent agreement. August groaned theatrically and slumped in his chair.

GÜLEN

Not even two class periods later, August was called into the office. He sat down nervously in a chair with peeling yellow paint and waited.

The dean stared at him for a couple of minutes, weighing him in the silence. He was an ex-marine: huge, mustached, and not known for his patience or leniency. Once he felt enough time had passed to sufficiently terrify August out of sheer suspense, he tossed a plastic bag on the desk. "Do you know anything about this?"

"No?"

The dean didn't look impressed. "Jason Matthews said he bought this from you. You can claim whatever you'd like, but the police are going through your locker. If we find something, there will be consequences."

August felt like someone was pouring cold water in a straight line slowly down his spine. There shouldn't be anything there. He hadn't gotten any fresh supply since Daliah had left for winter break. But what if they found some dust, or something had slipped out? There should be nothing. He never used his supply. *Never* opened the packages. He hadn't even known what half of them were.

August sat paralyzed with fear as the dean stared him down

wolfishly. The blood pounded in his ears with the ticking of the clock on the wall. When he'd gotten so anxious that it felt like he was about to vibrate right out of his skin, an officer stuck his head through the doorway.

"He's clean."

The dean steepled his hands over the desk. "Get out of my office."

#

#

#

BURN

August walked out of the office, down the stairs, and right out the front door. He just couldn't finish the day. And like always, he found himself in the woods. He quickly stacked some branches and fumbled in his coat for a matchbook. When the pile was finally lit, he shrugged off his backpack and curled up next to the fire.

Perhaps a bit too close.

Ash was getting on his face and in his hair.

The tension in his neck and shoulders was thick, tight from fear. He was so stressed out he wanted to cry. August looked at the flames and willed himself to stop shaking. This was the only thing that worked. Cigarettes couldn't really do this for him anymore. Sure, they were more portable, but they didn't work as fast as this did.

He wished he could share this feeling with Jack. He didn't even know what to call it. This melting, thawing, calming *burn*.

DON'T

"I told you, August. I told you."

August flicked ash into the ashtray by Rina's couch and stared at the wall. He'd thought he could escape a lecture by virtue of his mom not getting a call from the school, but he should have known better.

Jack scowled at him from across the room. "You can't ride on people's assumptions about you forever. Eventually, people are going to look past all your fancy clothes and neatness and notice what you're really like. You're lucky you got away with it this time. But it's just luck. You can't rely on it."

Rina watched them curiously from the kitchen as she sipped tea in her dressing gown. She never interrupted them when they got like this.

"And what am I 'really like,' Jack?" August shot back, fully understanding that he'd taken the bait. But he was past the point of caring. He'd just lost a large portion of his family's income, and he was not in the mood to get bitched out.

Jack sighed loudly in annoyance. "You're just . . . Fucking hell, August. You know what I mean." He gestured wildly. "On the out-side you're, like, pristine and neat and . . . you used to get a haircut every week for Christ's sake! But on the inside you're . . . that's not . . . well, you're not the same. That orderliness isn't there. I mean, at least you can tell from the outside that I'm batshit. At least it's not a fucking surprise. You're all complex and . . . you act like something is itching to crawl out of your skin."

August just stared at him.

"Something bad," Jack finished, looking absolutely wrecked.

There was silence. Then August put out his cigarette and got up from the couch and shrugged on his coat.

"No! No, wait, I didn't mean it like that. I just—" Jack reached out to pull him back, but August shrugged him off roughly and stalked toward the door. "August."

August stopped, his hand on the doorknob.

"I didn't mean . . . I mean . . . don't leave. Please."

August closed the door softly behind him.

STALEMATE

They didn't speak for a week. There were so many things August was mad about that he just *couldn't*. Jack showed up to his classes less and less before dropping completely off the radar by Wednesday.

August struggled not to care.

He had lots of distracting sex with Gordie, who seemed like she was trying to distract herself, too. He spent the rest of the time sleeping.

Saturday, though. Saturday was different. He could feel it prickling under his skin. What if Jack wasn't eating? Or sleeping? What if he was dead? It was so easy to think up terrible things. He could only be reassured if he saw him . . .

After a couple hours of stewing, August threw on his coat and hopped on his bike.

MY KINGDOM FOR A HORSE

August tossed his bike down on the lawn, dug out the key from the flowerpot, and let himself into Jack's house. All the lights were off. He walked through the living room and went upstairs to check for Jack—but no one was there.

"In the kitchen." Jack was waiting for him. Alone, sitting in the dark, with a mug of coffee on the table in front of him. He looked at August for a moment, then gestured for him to sit down. "So. You're back."

August settled into the chair. "I never left."

"That's not exactly true," Jack replied tartly. He rapidly tapped his fingers against the mug in agitation, but didn't say anything more. August stared down at the table. His throat was swelling with something. Embarrassment? No. It was shame. He could feel his cheeks getting hot. "Come here," Jack said.

August stood up and went to him.

"On the floor," Jack corrected. "I'm not going to look up at you. On your knees."

August sank down slowly until his knees hit the linoleum. He closed his eyes.

Jack was looking at him. He could feel it. "This is your game, August. *You* asked for it. And we aren't finished playing because you haven't asked to stop." Jack was close. His breath skittered across August's eyelids, making him shiver. "I'm sorry I made you angry. But don't ever run away from me. You shouldn't abandon your king. It's . . . dishonorable. Unchivalrous. Cowardly. You can't leave me behind," the Wicker King hissed.

And he was right. August couldn't leave him behind.

"Are you sorry?"

He nodded. He was sorry.

Jack crawled out of the chair and kneeled on the floor in front of him, but it no longer felt right for them to be on the same level. August felt himself bowing lower and lower until his forehead touched the floor.

August's pocket had been buzzing all through chemistry. He hadn't gotten a chance to check his cell phone yet, but chances were it was Gordie.

Earlier in the day, Alex had told him that Gordie was probably going to ask him to be her boyfriend again. She thought things were going well and wanted him to commit to a relationship.

And they *were* going well . . . in a way. They weren't fighting—which was a miracle—and he really liked having her around. But the entire concept of dating Gordie again gave him anxiety. It would be better to just step back now, before they reenacted their entire previous relationship.

She deserved a better guy than him. Someone who had time to actually take her on dates instead of ditching her all the time to deal with Jack.

And he *had* to deal with Jack. That was nonnegotiable.

When the bell rang, he took out his phone and answered whichever text was on the top without reading it:

we need to talk. 12:00 behind the gym

BRUT

"I don't think we should continue seeing each other," August said bluntly. He didn't like to beat around the bush. He was too tired for anything like that these days.

Gordie frowned. "Why?"

"I know you like me. Like, *like-like* me," August said. "And I'm sorry about that. You really shouldn't."

"Why?" she asked quietly. "Why shouldn't I?"

August looked down at the grass. He wasn't sure how to answer that question. "I didn't mean to lead you on. I didn't know you actually were interested in anything legitimate until Alex told me how you felt. I just can't right now. I'm sorry."

"You're so full of shit, August. You know exactly why I shouldn't. You're so choked up with your own hypocritical bull-shit that you can't even admit that you never liked me, or really wanted me at all."

"Gordie, I did like you. I do like you—"

Gordie laughed, harsh and angry. "And you know the best thing about it? I've always known you were like that and I loved you in spite of it. I thought, 'Maybe I could give him what he needs, even if I'm not the one he truly wants,' but—"

August stopped listening. What did she even mean by that? There was no other girl he wanted. He was way too busy to even consider something like that.

"And you didn't even have the decency to come at me like a man and give me the respect of admitting that you used me."

August rubbed his hand over his forehead. "I'm sorry. I'm just really tired right now. Okay? We can still be friends."

Gordie shook her head as she backed away from him. "No. No, we can't." She didn't even punch him good-bye.

DETENTION SLIP

Student _August Bateman_ Grade _12_

has been assigned detention:

Date(s) _1/17/03_ Time _2:30_ Room _105 B_

Reason for Detention _Sleeping in class._
When asked to sit up he refused
and gave the teacher the finger.

☐ Attended ☒ Did Not Attend

(Signature)

Jack leered at him, grinning dangerously.

"Don't hit as hard next time," August complained.

"I make no promises." Jack's hand twitched and August flinched. But he didn't move away.

"This feels like some sort of terrible trust exercise."

"You only say that because you're bad at this game. Besides, it's not my fault. If you moved away in time, you wouldn't get smacked."

August rolled his eyes dramatically, and Jack took the opportunity to whip his hands from under August's palms and slap the tops. Hard.

"Ow! Jesusfuckingchrist."

"Annnnnnd five out of five. I win," Jack said smugly.

August groaned and threw his hands up in the air. "Fine. Fine. I'll pay. But next time, I swear to god we're doing Rock Paper Scissors to decide instead of playing Hot Hands. Because it's not even fair that I have to pay for ice cream and deal with welts."

"Yeah, yeah, yeah. On with it, vassal." Jack smacked August's shoulder annoyingly as August rummaged for his wallet.

MILK

Watching Jack eat was one of August's least favorite activities. It was so awful, but once you got started, you couldn't stop staring at the mess. Jack slurped the bubble-gum ice cream dripping down his fingers. He followed the line all the way down his arm, licking shamelessly. He'd asked for a cone.

August had no idea why anyone would do such a thing. He neatly spooned his ice cream out of his cup and concentrated on looking dour.

"You seem happier than usual," Jack said.

"I'm actively frowning, Jack."

"*Pfft*, like that means anything. You frown all the time. Usually you have this extra rage wrinkle between your eyebrows, but it's gone now. What did you do?"

"I broke up with Gordie."

Jack looked way too excited about that information.

"What?"

"Nothing, nothing. I'm proud of you, man. She deserves better." Jack covered the entire top of his ice cream with his mouth and sucked hard.

August grimaced and looked away. "Yeah. She does."

GOD

They spent their afternoons with Rina every day now. They usually stopped by with snacks or dinner, then spread out on the floor to finish their homework. Her place was pretty great. It didn't have the hollow emptiness of Jack's giant house or the mild parental supervision of August's considerably smaller one. Plus, neither of their houses had a cute chick constantly puttering around.

August looked up from his history notes and watched as Rina bent down to rub some scuffing off her gold heels.

He felt Jack watching him watch her, so he turned to raise an eyebrow at him. But when he looked over, Jack was looking down at his book.

"Hey, Jack?"

Jack looked up, startled.

"Where are we now?" August asked.

"We're . . . on a hill. It's windy here, too, but I can't feel it. I can only see it waving through the grass."

"My apartment is on a hill?" Rina popped her head out of the kitchen to participate.

"You could say that," Jack said wryly.

"What else is out there?"

"Sheep," Jack replied instantly. "Or at least they look like they could be related to sheep. Too many horns."

"Jesus." Rina looked horrified. "How do you even get around?"

Jack picked at the carpet.

"You don't have to answer that if you don't want," August said softly.

Jack shrugged. "No, I don't mind. The only thing that's consistent now is people. I just watch the way everyone moves through a space and follow the paths. Plus, I've had at least three months to coordinate things. It's not as bad as it seems. And when that fails, I just follow him." He gestured at August.

August didn't meet his eyes.

NOTHING LEFT

Jack wanted to go to bed early, so they kissed Rina good-bye. Jack headed quickly down the stairs, but August paused at the doorway.

"Hey, weird question, but . . . why do you let us stay here?"

Rina crossed her arms and leaned against the doorframe.

"Why is it important? You're already here and I'm not saying no."

August laughed, but rubbed the back of his neck awkwardly. "I know, I know. But seriously. I've never . . . usually people don't just open up like this. Or do anything for . . . us."

Rina rolled back and forth on her heels and frowned. She wouldn't meet his eyes.

"Would it be weak if I said I was just lonely? It's hard to make friends after you leave school," she admitted.

"It's not weak," August said firmly.

He paused and looked over his shoulder to check for Jack, then pulled Rina into a quick hug.

"It's not weak. My mom once told me that being alone makes you feel weaker every day, even if you're not," he said quietly. "But it's not as bad if you're with other people who are alone, too. We can hold each other up like a card tower."

"Your mom sounds really smart," Rina murmured into the lapel of his jacket.

"Yeah." August smiled. "She's the best."

* My boys

TEN INCHES

August, Roger, and Peter had geometry together. They had spent the past couple of weeks subtly migrating across the room from their assigned seats until Roger sat in front of August and Peter sat to Roger's left, against the wall.

They passed notes. Predictably, Jack didn't like being discussed in public, which August had made the mistake of doing once. But now that they all ate lunch together and his afternoons were completely occupied, August had to figure out some way to update the twins while Jack wasn't there. This seemed to work pretty well.

Roger's main concern at the moment was making sure Jack and August were doing all right, whereas Peter was generally more interested in the progression of the prophecy.

I'm mostly curious about how the completion of the quest will affect his current state. I wonder if he'll get better or worse.

August scowled at him ferociously and wrote back: *Jack isn't an experiment. Stop talking about him like that.*

He received: *You don't have to get so butthurt.*

Before August could unleash all hell upon him, Roger snatched the note off his desk. "Ignore him," he said. "You're doing fine."

WARDEN

August went into the school library. He needed to return a couple of books. He'd started taking out more fairy-tale books for Rina because she'd exhausted the selection in her own town library. To his surprise, he spotted Gordie and Carrie-Anne sitting together, talking excitedly at a table in the back of the room.

They'd never been friends before. This was . . . startling.

In the past, Gordie had griped along with August about Carrie-Anne, but now she was riveted by whatever Carrie-Anne was saying, as if they'd been friends for years. Suddenly, she spotted August staring from across the room. Gordie said something, and then Carrie-Anne turned to look at him, too.

August waved and smiled—mostly out of reflex.

Gordie didn't wave back. Carrie-Anne frowned at him and turned back around. Whatever Carrie-Anne said next made Gordie laugh. Then Gordie grinned at him with open hostility, like she knew something he didn't. August tossed his books on the counter, scanned his ID, and got out of there as quickly as possible.

"It was creepy," August said, leaning his head back against the couch.

Rina clucked her tongue disapprovingly and continued running her fingers through his hair.

"I mean, normally Carrie-Anne wouldn't be caught dead near someone like Gordie. They're diametrically opposed. The only thing they have in common is that they both hate me."

"Also, Gordie was your . . . girlfriend—for lack of a better word. And Carrie-Anne was Jack's."

August thought for a moment. "Well, yeah. That doesn't make me feel better about them striking up a new hate-based companionship."

Rina squeezed his shoulders between her knees. "You're bad for girls, August. You're so pretty and smart and *devastatingly mysterious*, but you really don't care about anything outside of several very specific people. None of which include your woman du jour. Sometimes girls just like to decompress and gossip about boys they've dated. Especially if they feel slighted somehow. Give them some slack and let them have their fun. I'd be pissed, too."

"You think I'm pretty?" August asked, grinning. He tried to twist and look at her, but Rina grabbed his head and covered his eyes.

"Ugh. If your head swelled any more you wouldn't fit through doorways. Stop smiling, *sanam*, and go turn off the kettle. The tea should be ready."

His heart thrummed and swelled.

CICERO

Jack got there about a half hour later. He nearly tripped over the doorstop, but he caught himself and carried on. He was starting to get bruises all over from bumping into things he couldn't see.

He didn't bother to hide them. He didn't care.

"Oh my *God*, you would not believe the day I've had. I just want to sleep forever," Jack said, tossing his backpack next to the couch. He toed off his Chucks and collapsed to the floor, curling up next to August's knees.

"I'd like some mashed potatoes and a massage." He pouted.

"We all have wishes," August said absentmindedly. He'd decided not to tell Jack about Gordie and Carrie-Anne. There was already enough to worry about.

"You look thinner," Jack said suddenly.

August shrugged.

"You need to eat."

"I do. I'm just stressed out. Don't worry about it."

GLOOM

Rina got back from work late. She closed the door softly behind her. August gazed wordlessly at her silhouette in the yellow light of the landing. She put her purse and jacket in the coat closet and kicked off her sparkly heels.

Jack breathed softly in his sleep.

Rina turned and saw them. Sitting, tangled. She padded across the carpet.

Rina and August locked eyes.

Jack whimpered, beginning to wake up, and August instinctively pulled him closer. He didn't break his gaze, challenging her to say anything about it. Rina tilted her head to the side in contemplation and looked at them. Then, after a while, as if coming to some grand conclusion, she leaned down and kissed Jack gently on the cheek. August watched her, his mind filled with static.

Then Rina paused and leaned down to kiss him, too. Not on the cheek, like Jack had gotten, but full and real. Hungrily. Fingers plunging into his hair to hold him.

Then she pulled away, went into her room, and closed the door.

CRÈME

"So, do you like her?"

"Yeah, she gets me. Just like you said she would."

"Oh. Hmm . . ."

"What? Didn't you want this from the beginning?"

"Yeah, I did . . . Are you going to start dating her?"

August shrugged. "If that's what she wants."

"Is that what you want?"

"Is that what *you* want?" August shot back, laughing under his breath while he continued icing cupcakes. He'd been kidding—he hadn't noticed Jack flinch like he'd been slapped. His back to his king, broad and vulnerable.

"Do what you want. You know who you belong to." If the look on his face was anything to go by, Jack clearly regretted his words the moment they fell out of his mouth.

August put the spatula down and half turned to look at him. He smiled, always indulgent, even in the face of Jack's petulance. "Yeah. I know."

They fell into each other.

Five months ago, he probably would have been too nervous and overthought the entire thing. But now, all August could think about was the red smeared across her mouth and the delicate curve of her neck. He didn't have room for anything else.

Rina Medina, Queen of the Desert. Queen of the place between dishpan hands and Louboutins.

He fucked her hard.

She didn't ask for more.

It was weird, but it made him want to give her things. It made him want to cover her in diamonds. It made him want to work until he could afford to put her in a palace. It made him want to steal her away like a priceless work of art. It made him want to be selfish.

He never wanted to leave this little shack she called a home.

LINEN

Rina lay next to him as he smoked and stared out the window. She drummed her fingers restlessly on his knee.

"Sometimes," she said, "I get a craving for something. Something expensive or hard to find, like truffles. If I can't get them, I try for the next best thing. M&M'S, Snickers. Whatever. But no matter how much I have, it doesn't quite hit the spot . . ." She gazed over at him. "I don't mind being that for you."

"You're not. I don't know what you mean," August replied. "I try not to crave things I can't afford."

"You are a world-class liar, August Bateman. Every inch of you craves things you can't afford . . . or don't feel like you're allowed to have."

"Why are you being so vague?" he said impatiently. "Just tell me what you want to tell me, Rina. If you want something from me, all you have to do is ask."

She looked at him like he was mind-numbingly stupid. "Can't you see that's what I'm trying to tell you? I don't want anything from you. I never did. You were breaking his heart and the only thing that helped is watching you be happy. And I know that, and I'm okay with it. I've known it from the beginning. That's the entire reason that you're here. . . ."

August understood all those sentences separately, but they made no sense together.

"Why is this so confusing for you?" she asked. "What is wrong with you?"

Before he could answer, the doorknob rattled and turned, and the door swung open.

Jack stood there, filling up the doorway awkwardly. His eyes flicked over them, taking in Rina, who stared back at him boldly—nipples taut, hair loose and dark around her shoulders. He glanced for a second at the lighter in August's hand. Jack looked exhausted and like he was an instant away from bolting.

"Shh. Come here," August said quietly. Jack hesitated. "It's okay." August moved over and made space for him.

Jack glanced at Rina nervously as he crept into her bed, his sandy, cropped hair sticking up at odd angles. August took one last drag of his cigarette, then reached over Jack to put it out in the tray by the bed.

"Are you okay? Did anything happen?" Rina asked.

"No. I just . . ." Jack looked embarrassed. "My head hurts."

"Do you want me to get some aspirin?" August started to get up, but Jack curled closer and closed his eyes.

"No. No. I'm fine. Just don't go anywhere."

STRAIN

"You guys need to figure this out." Rina got out of bed and started putting on her uniform.

August sighed and continued running his hand over Jack's head. Jack had fallen asleep shortly after arriving.

"He's always been odd. It doesn't bother me. I've spent most of my life following him around, doing what he wants. So this isn't new either, even with . . . everything. It's just more dramatic."

"You love him." It wasn't said like a question.

August looked down at Jack's sleeping face and frowned. "I'm *responsible* for him. And I owe him. Knowing that he's okay is important to me. More important than anything else right now."

"I know you probably don't want to hear this, but I don't think that's healthy."

"Probably not," August said, but he didn't stay his hand.

SNAP

Jack was sleeping over. He'd forgotten one of his textbooks back at his house, so August hopped on his bike to go pick it up. It started to rain on the way.

August tossed his bike onto the lawn and went up to the door. He dug in his pocket for his keys, but something made him pause. Instead, he reached out and knocked.

Jack's father opened the door.

August hadn't seen this man in months. He looked just like Jack but older, more polished. He stood there in the doorway like he belonged there—like he was innocent—holding a glass of wine.

"Hi, August. Have you seen Ja—"

August punched him in the face. He hauled Jack's father inside and smashed him against the wall, scrunching the older man's sweater in his fists. "Where have you been, you son of a bitch?"

"Let go of me!"

"He waited for you. You're his father. You're his *father*! You're supposed to be there for him."

"You can't tell me how to raise my ch-child," Jack's father stammered. He had gray eyes like Jack's.

August let go of him in disgust and stepped back, throwing out his arms. "Oh yeah? And who do you think has been raising him while you were gone? This is bullshit and you know it. And

Christmas? *Christmas?* You're lucky I don't smash your head open on the sidewalk."

Jack's father slumped against the wall, staring at August in horror and rage. He clutched his bleeding nose with one hand, unsuccessfully trying to keep the blood from dripping on his shirt. "Get off my property or I'm calling the police," he spat.

August was already halfway up the walk. "We'll be back for the rest of Jack's shit in the morning."

SOVEREIGN

August was so mad he was shaking. He tried to calm down before he got back home, but it just wasn't working. He kept remembering that smug bastard's face. Anger pounded in his head and blurred his vision.

"Your dad is back." August slammed the door open. "You're moving in. We're getting your stuff in the morning."

Jack looked up at him calmly. "What did you do?"

"I fulfilled a promise."

There was a moment as Jack figured out what that meant. August waited. Water dripped from his hair and clothes and soaked into the carpet.

They both breathed.

Finally, the Wicker King rose and crossed the room.

August sank to his knees before him. His fists were still tight and angry, ready on his thighs. He gritted his teeth, and again, he waited.

A hand passed over his face, slicing through his hair for a bit, then ran past his ear to cup his jaw. August couldn't remember when he'd closed his eyes, but the dark was deep and clear and sharp.

"*Well done.*"

It echoed in his bones like it had been spoken by giants,

spoken by *gods*. Nothing could replace the glory of the Wicker King's favor—the peace of returning from defending his honor. The phrases that ran through his mind were archaic and ridiculous *and urgent* and more real than anything he'd ever known.

August tilted his head to brush his lips against his king's hand, reaffirming his loyalty. The rage was gone now. It had served its purpose.

"Look at you."

August opened his eyes and it was just Jack again, a boy without his crown. Staring down at him in something like wonder and something like fear.

PILLOW

August's phone buzzed off the nightstand and fell to the floor. He slid off the bed and reached around blindly to pick it up. It was a text from Roger. August sighed loudly and flopped over, nearly elbowing Jack in the face.

> my mom is back from Prague. you should come
>> by and see her
> did u tell her?

He sent it quickly and rubbed his eyes. The prospect was sobering.

"What are you doing? Why is it so bright?" Jack complained tiredly, burrowing closer to the wall.

"Roger's texting me. He wants me to meet their mom so I can talk to her about you."

> no. I didn't. I told you I wouldn't but you should still come
>> anyway. you haven't been looking so great lately. you
>> shouldn't have to deal with this by yourself

Jack turned over to watch what was going on.

> dnt worry abt me, roger

"Roger's worried about me," August whispered.

Jack smiled sleepily. "He's nicer than he seems."

"Yeah."

> just think about it
> noted. Thnx

YOU'LL NEVER KNOW, DEAR

Rina sat up suddenly. "I made you something." She dashed into the kitchen, turned off the kettle quick, then ducked into her bedroom. August got up and began pouring their tea into mugs. He took one in each hand and settled down by the couch.

She scampered into the room with one hand behind her back. "Close your eyes."

He did.

Rina took their mugs from him and placed them neatly on the floor. Then she straddled him and made a place for herself on his lap. He put his hands on her hips and opened his eyes. She pressed a CD hard against the side of his face.

"I didn't say you could open them yet! You're terrible at following instructions, August. Ugh. Anyway. Don't laugh, but I made you a mixtape."

August kissed her knuckles, kissed her forehead, kissed her cheek, then kissed her mouth, rubbing his nose against hers, grinning. He plucked the CD from her hands and tossed it across the room toward his backpack.

"Thank you."

"I didn't know what music you liked and I was feeling cliché and sentimental."

"About little old me? We getting hitched now?" August tucked a finger under her bra strap and snapped it. Rina pinched him back.

"Shut up. What's your favorite song?" she asked, tugging his shirt over his head.

"'Gloria' done by the great Patti Smith."

Rina crinkled her nose in distaste.

"What's Jack's?"

August smirked. "'You Are My Sunshine.'"

"Really? That's so weird," she squeaked as August ran his fingers like spiders up her sides. He began tickling her in earnest, grinding against her as she laughed and tried to pry off his jeans.

"*He's* weird. But let's not talk about him right now."

ONE EIGHT-HUNDRED

Roger began texting him every day. Usually it was some version of *Are you okay?* but sometimes he'd text things that made August laugh, like *Peter hates red peppers. Made dinner and put them in anyway.* Or weird questions like *How did we all decide that clapping is a good way to let people understand appreciation with a nonverbal cue?* and *What is scarier, one large scary thing or many, many small scary things?*

August wasn't nearly as comedic himself, and he usually just answered pretty straightforwardly. But it was fun.

"You're probably his first real friend outside of Peter," Jack said.

August closed his phone and shoved it back into his pocket. "Well, there's that, but I think he's also checking up on me. He's just being really casual about it."

Jack shrugged. "Why is that a bad thing? As long as he doesn't tell, it will be fine. I'm pretty sure at this point, if they told anyone, I'd be taken away from my parents for, like, severe negligence or something. Keep texting him back."

"Yeah, yeah."

BLACK-BODY RADIATION

August was sitting in the woods decompressing when the hairs suddenly rose on the back of his neck.

"So. This is what you do when I'm not around."

August moved to try to hide the fire, kicking damp dirt and leaves over it. But Jack just laughed anyway and clapped him on the shoulder.

"It's okay, really. We all have our vices and secrets. What are you, a pyromaniac now?" Jack was smiling. It wasn't a nice smile.

"No, I just—"

"You just like making small fires all over the woods every week? You're not subtle, August. I figured it out pretty quickly. Is this how you get by with dealing with me and my little problem?"

"No, that's not what—"

"Be quiet," Jack said harshly. August fell silent. "I don't . . . I can't understand why you . . ." Jack covered his mouth, then crossed his arms as he tried to decide what to say.

August couldn't meet his eyes. The weight of Jack's disappointment choked him.

"Can you stop?"

"I . . . I don't know."

Jack laughed again and shook his head. Then he turned on his heel and walked away.

Jack stopped walking. He slid his hand over August's arm, pulling him back from the trees in front of them.

"What?"

"Shh. It will hear you," Jack breathed. August looked at the empty forest, then turned back and watched his friend instead.

Jack's nails bit into his skin. "Shit. *Shit.* It sees us. Fuck. *RUN.*" He bolted, dragging August along with him.

They crashed through the forest toward the town, leaping over fallen trees and dodging branches. August's arm slipped out of Jack's grasp, but he charged on because Jack was clearly running for his life.

"Come *on*, August. I can't lose you, I can't—" They were neck and neck now and August could just barely see the road through the trees. He slipped in the mud and fell hard.

"*No!*" Jack roared. He leaped in the air and kicked off one of the trees, curling his arm around the trunk and spinning himself in a stunning feat of desperate athleticism. Changing trajectory completely, he sprinted to August and pulled him up.

They flew toward the light.

Jack let out a cry when they burst out onto the open road. They both skidded to a stop. August couldn't breathe. His heart was beating so fast that he felt like he was dying. Jack staggered a couple of meters ahead of him, looking up at the sky, panting just as hard.

"What . . . the fuck . . . What did you see?!"

Instead of answering, Jack gazed down at his hand. There were deep scratches from the tree bark, and they were starting to bleed.

"Jack. Fucking . . . tell me what's . . . going on!"

"WOULD YOU JUST BE QUIET FOR A SECOND. Just a second . . . *please*." He sank to the ground and covered his eyes with his hands, smearing his face with blood. He was shaking terribly.

August knelt before him and pulled him to his feet. "Come on. I'll take you home."

"It was horrible. It looked like a bison, but at least five times bigger. It was half rotten and its skin was hanging sloppily off its body. Its bottom jaw stretched all the way to the ground, and there was still meat stuck between its teeth. I don't think I've ever been more scared in my fucking life." Jack drank straight from the bottle of wine. When he put it down, Rina snatched it from him.

"The worst thing of all was that when it finally turned to look at us, its eyes were almost human. Like, you know, that part in the His Dark Materials series, in the third book where—never mind. Anyway, it was like it was smart. Like it could probably have talked if its jaw wasn't a gigantic gaping maw of rotting razor-sharp death."

"So I'm assuming this is the first time you've ever seen one of those," August said dryly. He was still exhausted from having to sprint half a mile with absolutely no warning.

Jack glared at him. "You know what this means, right? It means *we're running out of time.* Quests always have an ending, whether it's a good one or a bad one. Always."

August looked thoughtful. "I wonder what would have happened if I'd just let it get me," he mused, rubbing his chin.

"We're not figuring that out."

"Why?" August insisted.

"Because we're just *not*, you insufferable asshole."

"I mean technically, I can't touch anything in your world. Chances are, it wouldn't be able to touch me either."

"What if? I just had to watch you get violently eaten? Then I completely lost the ability to see you? What about that?" Jack spat angrily.

August went silent.

August rested his forehead on the knob of Rina's spine as she angrily did the dishes.

"You need to take him to the hospital," she whispered.

"I know," August said.

"I can't be held responsible for this anymore. I won't have him drinking in my home to escape this."

"He won't, I promise. He barely ever drinks. He was just scared."

Rina whirled around, eyes blazing. "If he's your responsibility, you should be responsible enough to fix it. If you're looking after him, look after him," she whispered furiously.

"What do you think I'm doing?" August shot back.

"I think you're doing your best," Rina said, tossing the wet dishrag into the sink. "But your best is not good enough some-times," she said, deflating a bit. "Sometimes . . . you have to stop trying and just let someone else try their best. In order to survive."

It was the worst thing August had ever heard. He took a deep breath and closed his eyes. When he opened them, he could see that she knew what he was going to say before it came out of his mouth.

"We can handle it. He won't drink anymore. Thank you for your concern."

Then he walked out of her kitchen and took Jack home.

BRAVE

SOMEONE FUCKING HELP ME
XXV

WATER

August turned over and blinked blearily in the early light. He frowned. Jack was sitting up, wide awake, and looking out the window. "Did you ever get to sleep?"

"No."

August sighed. "Are you still upset about yesterday?"

"No. I don't care about that anymore. I've been thinking. I think I've figured out how to fulfill the prophecy."

"What do you want me to do?"

Jack was silent.

"Just tell me what you want. And stop looking so scared. I'm not going to say no."

"We can do it with either fire or water. Fire, you're familiar with, so that shouldn't be a problem. Water . . . water is what I'm worried about. There are two ways to make it so you can affect things on the other side. The first is manually: we create a large enough energy source around the Rapturous Blue to jump-start it. Or alternatively, by baptizing you. Ritually."

August laughed nervously. "The water one sounds easier."

"We have to drown you," Jack continued bluntly. "Or just nearly enough that you pass through the gates, but not so much that you can't come back from there. To face what is beyond this world, so you can be allowed to play in mine."

August looked at Jack. Really looked at him. He looked weak.

Thoroughly spent. His skin under his eyes seemed so thin that it looked almost bruised. "Is this what you want?"

"I don't want it. I don't want for you to . . . But I think that maybe the visions will end if we . . ." Jack swallowed hard.

"I'll do it," August promised. "I'll do it. Come here, go to sleep. Don't worry about it. I'll do it."

ROSEMARY AND THYME

As soon as they got to the lunchroom, Jack stacked his books in a makeshift pillow and promptly went to sleep. August stirred his macaroni and cheese mindlessly and stared out the window.

"You guys look awful," Peter proclaimed.

"You're talking?" Alex said, in completely justified shock.

Peter narrowed his eyes at her. "We *can* talk, we just don't like to. But I thought it would be good to let August hear, verbally, how absolutely terrible and tired he looks. Like he's had all the life sucked out of him . . . by . . . something. But I can't imagine what it could be," Peter said sassily. He popped a cherry tomato in his mouth and absorbed August's glare with practiced indifference.

To August's surprise, Roger didn't even temper his brother. Instead, he reached out and put his hand over August's so he would stop vigorously stirring his food.

"Your time is running out," Roger said gently.

"No one is supposed to get hurt. Not even you," Peter scoffed.

Alex stared at them all, fiddling with her glasses in suspicion. "Am I missing something? What's going on?"

"Nothing." August shook Roger's hand off his. "We're fine."

DETENTION SLIP

Student _August Bateman_ Grade _12_

has been assigned detention:

Date(s) _Jan 29, 2003_ Time _12:50_ Room _102_

Reason for Detention _When asked to_
produce hmwrk screamed "What do you
all want from me." And left class
without a hall pass.

☐ Attended   ☒ Did Not Attend

_____
(Signature)

TIGHT

August shut the classroom door behind him, ignoring Mrs. Sirra's angry shouting, and walked quickly down the hallway. He couldn't breathe. He couldn't *breathe*. His heart slammed against his rib cage like it was trying to leap out onto the linoleum. He stopped and leaned against the lockers near the gym, gasping for air. Sliding to the floor, he pressed his face against the cold metal.

He'd seen his mom have these. It was just a panic attack. He wasn't dying, it was just a panic attack. They always passed. They were designed to pass.

The hallway swam before his eyes, so he closed them. August couldn't afford to leave school early today. He had history next and he was only 3 percent away from getting a solid D. His GPA was already lower than it had ever been in his entire life, but getting less than a 3.0 was not an option if he wanted to go to college.

August pressed his cheek against the locker harder, squeezed his eyes so tight that tears leaked from the corners, and concentrated on getting his heart rate down.

He could do this. It was just school. School was easy. He could make up work. He could send out apologetic e-mails. He could ask for more time. He could settle for less than his best. He could do this. All he had to was get up and breathe and finish the day.

Everything was going to be fine.

August pulled himself to his feet and lurched into the bathroom. He dug his lighter out of his backpack and flicked it on and off and on and off until the skin closest to the flames ran hot. Until his heart slowed down and he could see shapes dancing in the light. Until he could breathe again.

And suddenly, with a jolt of horror, he realized that he couldn't live without it anymore.

It was as much a part of him as anything now. He couldn't run from it any more than anyone could run out of their own skin. It would just keep coming back, over and over, curling up out of him, growing like hunger. He would crave the burn until he was dead. August curled up against the wall and put his head in his arms.

He gripped the lighter so tightly that his knuckles went white.

<u>In-School Suspension Exit Slip</u>

Name	Date	Supervising Teacher	Homeroom Teacher
August Bateman			

I served an in-school suspension because _i burned a book in the_ _parking lot_

From this incident, I learned … _not burn books in the parking lot?_

If I am faced with this situation again, I will _not burn a book in_ _the parking lot._

I believe this is a better decision because _i wouldn't be doing this form._

To be their "Barnard Best" I think all students should:

1. _come to class_
2. _sit quietly in class_
3. _not burn books_
4. _____
5. _____

Please use this exit slip to complete a letter, on the reverse side, to a fellow student explaining positive choices they can make throughout the day. Try to be an encouragement to others by giving specific examples of how to be their "Barnard Best."

Student Signature: _AB_   Date: _____

The new grass tickled August's cheek as they lay in the field, their coats and backpacks strewn around them.

"Tell me about the prophecy again."

"Only if you eat this apple."

August frowned at the request, but snatched it from Jack's hand and took a large bite.

"Basically, the Wicker King, which is me, must return to the citadel as one-half of the prophecy. And the Wicker King's knight and champion, which is you, must put the Rapturous Blue on the stand. Without both parts, the Cloven King has access to an unclaimed throne and there is no protection against the darkness and his horde of life-draining wraiths. Or whatever. Plus, not to worry you or anything, but if we don't work on this, the influence of the citadel will spread and this world will be shrouded in despair until the end of time."

"Okay . . . Now tell me about the fire."

Jack waved something August couldn't see away from his face, then continued. "It's not so much fire we need, but an energy source. The Rapturous Blue doesn't care if it's free energy or destructive energy, only that there is enough of it to jump-start it. We could use electricity, but that's a bit too complicated. We'd likely need about a bolt of lightning's worth, and as much as I'd love to risk getting shocked to death, I wouldn't want to see you accidentally killed." Jack grinned softly at that. "Fire is a good substitute because the energy to destroy is wild, rampant, and cheap. We just need to figure out a way to create a decent amount of it."

"We could burn a building." August chewed contemplatively. "We could burn the toy factory around the stand."

Jack rolled his eyes. "Yeah. Except that's *arson*. Why can't we just burn a bunch of stuff in the woods?"

"Do you really want to intentionally start a forest fire? It will spread to the town. They'll put us away forever."

"And they *won't* if we burn down a whole fucking building?"

"Dude. The toy factory is abandoned. It's been abandoned for more than twenty years. No one cares." August lazily tossed the apple core to the side and flopped over.

Jack nodded slowly after he thought awhile. "Okay. . . Okay. If the water doesn't work, we'll do that. Whatever. We just need to hurry. The city is getting darker as he pushes closer to the citadel, and it's wearing on me. The imperial hornets are coming out of the woodwork. We don't have much more time."

August didn't know what that meant, but still, he trembled.

THREAD COUNT

August went downstairs and sat next to his mom on the futon. *The Price Is Right* was on. The television was loud and abrasive and he wished he could just smash the thing against the wall. "I have a question."

She *hmm*ed, but didn't even blink.

"Would you do something bad if you knew it would have more good in it, in the end, than bad?"

"What's good is good and what's bad is bad," she murmured, fiddling with the corner of her quilt.

August gritted his teeth in frustration, but he continued in a soft voice. "I have to do something important. And dangerous—"

"Is it for Jack?" she interrupted.

"Oh. Um. Yeah," August said, surprised.

"You think I don't notice things. But I do."

SEMPER FIDELIS

"Are you scared?"

"No."

"Yes, you are. But you're very brave, too . . ." Jack fidgeted anxiously as he sat on the edge of the tub. "I understand now why they chose you over me. Why the council wanted you as their champion, and why I was unfit."

August turned on the tap.

"They have stories about you, songs. They call you the Raven, the Golden Bird, the King's Lionheart. Women smile at you as we walk in the streets; men talk about you over their fires. It's written all over the walls. They love you and you can't even *see* them . . . my *Lionheart*. Can you imagine?"

Jack steadfastly kept his eyes on the tile as August pulled off his shirt and jeans, dropping them in a heap in the corner. He stepped gingerly into the tub and lay down in the water, his boxers soaking through.

"I hope this works," Jack sighed.

August sat up suddenly and gripped Jack's forearm. "I am doing this for you. Not the Wicker King. Not what we have become. But for *you*. If anything goes wrong, I want you to remember that."

Jack nodded. August slipped beneath the water—and breathed.

CLEAR

He came to. Hacking water onto the tile. His nose was bleeding. The room tilted and whirled. Distantly, he could feel Jack brushing his hair back from his forehead, frantically trying to help.

August pinched his nose until the flow stopped, then collapsed to the floor in exhaustion. Jack pulled him up and cradled him in his arms.

"Did you see anything?" he asked, sounding both terrified and hopeful.

August swallowed. His chest burned and spasmed. It took him a minute to answer, though he valiantly kept trying to get the words out. "No," he choked. "I'm sorry."

Jack curled around him, pressing their foreheads together in sorrow. They breathed the same air. So close but not touching. Never touching. Through the haze, August wondered if Jack could taste the remnants of stardust he'd brought back with him from the edge of death.

"It's okay," he whispered. "Everything is going to be okay."

TARTARUS

They went to school the next day as if nothing had happened. August had a test in math. Jack slept though British Literature.

Alex and the twins said nothing about the bruises under August's eyes.

Or the way his hands shook when he picked up his water.

Or how his food sat on his tray, untouched, for the third time that week.

August burned a paperback book out in the parking lot again because his hands had begun shaking uncontrollably from stress, and he couldn't find anything else on such short notice. He was more careful this time, though, and managed not to get caught. Afterward he doused the fire with Coke, put his backpack on, took a breath, and went back inside.

BLUEBERRY

The next day August woke up to his doorbell ringing. That hadn't happened in . . . years. Even the mailman just knocked and left packages on the doorstep. August crept downstairs suspiciously and peered through the keyhole. To his surprise, Alex was standing on his doorstep. He barely saw her outside of school, much less at his actual house. He opened the door and leaned against the frame.

"Hey . . . what are you doing here?"

Alex was holding a box and looked uncomfortable. She pushed the box into his arms and flipped the top open. "I made you some muffins," she blurted.

"Thank you . . . It's not my birthday?" He picked one up and smelled it. They had to be home baked, they were still warm.

"I know we're not really close. And that's totally fine; this isn't some weird bribery gift or anything. I have enough friends." Alex wrung her hands. "I just wanted to make something for you that you would like? You don't seem very . . . I mean, it's not my place to say anything about it or criticize you . . . I know I'm hardly perfect, and I just . . . I . . . don't know what's going on in your life, but you don't seem . . . okay? And I just wanted you to know that if you ever ever *ever* need anything, you can come to me about it."

"Wow . . . Thank you," August said quietly, holding the box a bit closer.

"Okay, I'm going to walk away now. This is probably the most awkward thing I've ever done."

August took a bite of one of the muffins as he watched her scamper down his front walk. They were delicious. Perfect in every way. "Hey, Alex?" She turned around. "You're a true MVP."

Alex grinned.

GOLD

August knocked on Rina's apartment door. She opened it only halfway and stood in the entrance, blocking him from coming inside.

She looked radiant. Her hair was piled on her head in a messy nest. She was wearing boxers and a frumpy gray sweatshirt. Her lips were painted brilliant red.

"Hey," she said curtly before he could say anything. "I've made a decision."

August rocked back on his heels and put his heavy backpack on the floor. "Okay. What is it?"

Rina drummed her nails against the wooden frame of the doorway. "I'm not going to let you guys come here anymore. I'm just helping to make a space for the both of you to think that all of this is okay. I don't want to be an enabler. It's not fair. You need to get him help, August. You can't come back here until you get him help."

August swallowed hard and looked down at his shoes.

"It doesn't make you a bad friend," she said softly. "It doesn't mean you love him less. It doesn't mean I love you any less."

Rina took his hand and squeezed it, then tugged him close and let him bury his face in the curve of her neck. August snaked his arms around her waist and held her tight for as long as he could. Then he picked up his backpack and swung it onto his shoulders.

"We'll come back. I promise." August's voice cracked. "When we see each other again, things will be different."

Rina touched his cheek and guided his head down so they were level. Then she kissed him gently on the forehead. "They had better."

BRICK

August jolted awake with a gasp.

"Dude. Picture day." The kid sitting behind him stopped flicking the back of his neck once he saw that August wasn't asleep anymore. "We all have to go to the gym—they just announced it on the intercom. Why aren't you dressed in nice clothes?"

August looked around. The kid was right. Pretty much everyone was in dress shirts and ties, and the girls were in dresses. He looked down at his stretched-out shirt. With all the commotion lately, he'd completely forgotten about picture day. It was just so irrelevant in the grand scheme of things that it had barely even crossed his mind that it would be around this time of year.

There was nothing to be done about it now. So August just sighed and sullenly followed the rest of his classmates down the hall and into the gym. Roger and Peter quickly spotted him and made their way through the crowd.

"Is that the best you could do?" Peter said derisively, looking at August's clothes.

"I forgot. I've been busy," August replied, pulling at his shirt. He was a little embarrassed. Peter smacked his hand away and began fiddling with August's hair.

"Don't pull on your shirt. You're making it worse. You're lucky you have a good haircut, at least." Peter fussed with him, scowling. August was so exhausted that he just let it happen.

Roger rummaged around in his backpack a bit. "I brought you some samples. Antianxiety meds, sleeping pills, what do you want?"

"I don't want your drugs, Roger, but thanks for offering. I just want to take my picture and go to class so I can get back to sleep," August mumbled.

Peter put his hands down and stared at August helplessly. "Well. That's the best we can do. They're making us line up in alphabetical order, so we have to go and get in the back. See you later." The twins walked away, but not without Roger sending August one of the most profound looks of pity he'd ever received in his entire life.

August clenched his hands into fists and stepped into line.

FLASH

"So, do you want the gray background or the black background?"

"Black."

The light was so bright, August's eyes could barely focus. He squinted at the camera.

"Sit up straight and smile!"

Yeah, he wasn't doing that. August took the opportunity to try to search Jack out near the back of the line to see how he was doing.

"Seriously, kid. You only get one shot."

Oh, he found him. Jack was up against the wall, hand outstretched to guide himself forward. Leaning into the warmth of the person in front of him to sightlessly follow the pattern of the line. People bumped into him and he crumpled under their force, unprotected. Like a small white boat being tossed in the black waves of a rolling sea. August's heart seized at the sight.

"I *said*, you're done."

He stumbled down from the chair and started toward the Wicker King like he was being pulled forward by an invisible rope. But before he could get there, his English teacher blocked his path.

"All students must sit on the bleachers until the rest of the class is finished."

August shook his head to clear his mind and rubbed at his eyes. "Oh. Okay. Sorry." He went to go sit on the bench with the others.

THE CLOVEN KING RISES

August had detention that day, so he didn't get out of school until late. He trudged home tiredly. But before he could even make it all the way inside the house, he heard the screams. He sprinted up the stairs and threw his bedroom door open. Nothing. He ran into the bathroom, where he found him. Jack was shuttered in a corner, curled as small as he could make himself, with his arms over his head. August threw himself into Jack, prying his arms up roughly and checking for injuries. He glanced back through the door and briefly considered if this was bad enough to disturb his mom about.

"August! August!" Jack shrieked as he clawed August's back and arms.

"Jack! Calm down!" he shouted over the hysteria to no avail. Part of him wanted to push Jack away, run downstairs, and call the emergency room, but another part wanted to clutch Jack to him and join in his panic. "Jack!" August grabbed him by the back of the neck and gripped hard, digging his nails into the skin. "Jack, stop!"

"Noo . . ." Jack shuddered with terror. *"Please."*

"What is happening?! WHAT ARE YOU SEEING?"

"They're standing around you," Jack whispered, his eyes wide and blind. "Ten of them. Dressed in black. They're speaking to me, but I can't hear them. It doesn't work that way. I can't hear them and they're changing the world. *My* world. And I can't change it back . . ."

"What are they changing it to?" August asked, gripping Jack's face between his hands. "Jack! You have to tell me what's going on!"

Jack sank to the floor in unspeakable melancholy, dragging August down with him. "I don't know," he sobbed. "I don't know."

LOVE

They awoke on the bathroom floor. Jack's face was still stained salty from the night before. He lifted his head and looked at August critically. August stared back at him, exhausted.

"You're so thin . . . ," Jack said. "You haven't been eating."

August swallowed. His throat burned like he'd been gulping down steel wool. He closed his eyes against the look on Jack's face. His head felt so heavy.

"August, you have to eat," Jack urged. He raised his fingers to August's lips and brushed his fingertips across them, his skin catching on the dryness. "You're going to die," Jack gasped shakily. He sounded scared again.

"So are you," August whispered. "We can't live this way, Jack. We have to tell someone. We're just . . . kids."

Jack laid his head back onto August's leg, and August weakly dropped his hand onto Jack's cheek. He closed his eyes again, drowning in the black. "I'm sorry."

"Don't be."

They skipped school that day. August brought a box of Pop-Tarts upstairs and they ate them in his bed. He was too tired to cook. Jack finished his first, then resumed staring off into nothingness.

"So . . . fire," he said after a while.

"Fire," August agreed.

"You kept that lighter I gave you? All this time, you didn't lose it."

"Yeah."

Jack laughed. "How romantic. My knight in shining fucking armor."

August's cheeks burned. "It's not that big of a deal. It's just a lighter," he mumbled.

Jack gazed at him for a moment. "Is anything 'just' anything? After all these months? Even dressed in my colors? Even with your favor at my feet? Even as the sky falls and the only thing I can hear besides your voice is the screams of the dying and the thundering of horses? You remembered to keep it when you couldn't even remember to eat. It's a lighter, yeah. But it's also everything . . ." Jack grinned. "We've had our conduit all along."

August gazed out the window. His neighbor was walking her dog. The bus was dropping off elementary school kids. An airplane flew overhead. The sky was so blue.

Jack reached out and grabbed August's chin, wrenching his face away from the light. "You burn things all the time these days," Jack said softly. "Would you burn for me?"

August stared him down. Stared into the gray of Jack's eyes. So clear, they were—not a hint of delusion. Just fierce and grand as the day he lay with his back in the river's mud. Ten thousand years ago.

"You already know I'll do it," August said.

You already know. You fucking know.

HOUSTON

August put the gasoline can down and waited. Jack lit his cigarette, holding it between strong white teeth before passing it over. Like a secondhand kiss on a breath of ash.

"Should I do it from the outside in?"

"Do it however, just make sure it's done."

"Will you come with me?" August asked quietly, blowing smoke into the wind.

"Do kings march out to war?"

"They used to."

He could feel Jack smiling at him. Breathed it in so he could feel it deep in his lungs. This was it. This was everything.

"Your kingdom come. Your will be done."

THE FIRE

He clipped the wiring to the alarm system and fire sprinklers with a knife.

August took care of the outer rooms first, setting tables and chairs in the offices alight. He splashed the doors and left them open.

Then he took to the perimeter of the factory floor. He went around the main room in a circle, dousing it all in gasoline. It was taking a while. The fire was beginning to break glass and consume wood. He would have to be quicker. August took the Rapturous Blue out of his backpack, wrapped it in the oilcloth Jack had given him, and set it on the floor.

It burned purple and indigo just as Jack had said it would, just like Jack had seen with his crazy eyes, just like it was *supposed to*.

He picked it up and put it in the water cooler, ignoring the blazing heat as the flames burned through his gloves, blistering his skin. Then he peeled them from his hands and dropped them to the floor.

August looked around him at the red and the orange and the yellow and the black and the Rapturous Blue that shone so bright, *finally* pulsing with purpose.

The serum from his raw, blistered palms sizzled as it dripped from his hands; he knew that it was worth it.

WELL

August kicked out the glass and came tumbling through the window. Jack caught him before he hit the ground and pulled him to his feet.

"You did it! You did it!" Jack was delirious in his happiness. He grasped August's wrists, beaming in the light of the flames.

The Wicker King was beautiful—brilliant, mad, sick, free. He kissed the blisters on the palms of August's hands. "Thank you. Thank you . . ."

August buried his face in Jack's chest, curling in against him to hide from the heat of the flames. Jack held him just as tight, fingers digging into his shoulders, his arms wrapping around August's waist, clutching at his hair. August didn't realize he was crying until his sobs began to choke him. "Is it over? Is it over? Is it over?" He wasn't talking about the fire.

"Hush," Jack murmured. "You did well." He rocked August gently back and forth. "You did well."

IRON AND ASH

The police wrenched them apart an hour later as the firefighters put out the flames.

Being snatched from Jack's grasp damaged his clarity. In the gray, there was the sound of shouting, men in masks and gloves, police officers with their rough hands and calm, stern voices. They took him and put him in the back of an ambulance, and Jack was taken aside for questioning. The paramedics kept repeating something to August, and he nodded blearily as they loosely bandaged his hands.

Someone was yelling at Jack and Jack was yelling back.

People were pushing August, pulling him, moving him, cuffing him, and locking him in the back of a squad car. He couldn't remember the drive at all. The haze remained until they slammed the door of the holding cell shut. Then everything became crisp all at once, and there was nothing left to filter out except the sounds of the other men in the cell with him.

HOLE

They sat an inch from each other. August scratched his bandaged fingers against the floor. "The kingdom?"

"Rejoicing," Jack said, staring sightlessly toward the wall.

"The throne?"

"Claimed."

"The people? The wraiths?"

"Safe, gone, denied."

August scratched again, the concrete scraping against his nails. "You still see it all, don't you?"

"As clear as I see you." Jack's head lolled against the cinder block, eyes unblinking. They sat like old marionettes with the strings cut at the root. Thrown carelessly to the ground to rot in the sun and dust. "Are you proud, Eagle of the North? The Champion with Sparks in his Veins. They will sing songs of your victory and word of your sacrifice will drip from the tongues of young and old until . . . the end of time. Are you proud?"

"Shut up," August said, curling in on himself on the cell floor. "Just shut up."

CELL BLOCK 3

The next night the cell was crowded. When they'd arrived, there were maybe five or six other people, but tonight there were at least fifteen. He and Jack had slowly migrated to the corner so they were out of sight behind a large, old drunk man who was slumped over and drooling on his leg in his sleep.

Jack had stayed away from August since the moment they arrived at the station, like he was afraid that touching him would break some sort of spell. It had bothered August at the time.

But now August was just angry at himself and numb. He knew his mom wouldn't come for him. And Jack's parents were probably out of state.

He gazed over at Jack, who was shivering and trying not to bring attention to himself. A man across the cell was leering at him.

"Jack," he whispered. "Come here."

Jack twisted toward him, startled.

August opened his arms.

After a moment's hesitation, Jack leaned down and rested his head against August's knee. Very stiffly, as if he didn't belong there.

August flinched as one of the men in the room said something derogatory and vulgar about the nature of their relationship, but his hand was steady as it rested against Jack's neck.

"*You are my sunshine. My only sunshine. You make me happy* when skies are gray." He hummed the next bit because he didn't know the words.

GREEN

His lawyer was a woman, and he thanked fuck that it was a woman who had sons.

"If you plead guilty, you'll probably get some community service and a fine at best and a year in prison at worst," she said, taking a sip of her coffee. "You torched the place with gasoline. A jury isn't going to believe it if you plead innocence."

"Is there any way I can plead insanity?" August asked tentatively.

She put the cup down and gave him a look. "Why on earth would you want to do that?"

"Because that's what Jack is going to do. He's unstable. He can't hide it anymore. Plus, if we both plead the same thing, there is a chance that we'll be sent to the same place. I don't care how slim it is, it's worth it."

She pursed her lips and drummed her fingernails on the table as she thought about it. "What is the nature of your relationship? I know you were living together at the time of the incident."

"We're not dating, if that's what you're asking," August sighed. "We're just friends, I think. We grew up together. His mom and my mom were really close when we were kids, before my parents' divorce. So we have just always been together."

"I have kids myself. Three boys . . . they're not much younger than you." She shook her head and laughed to herself a bit. "I can almost understand . . . but do you mind if I ask a question? Why did you do it? You don't have any prior offenses. Your grades were pristine until this semester. It all seems so uncharacteristic. What happened?"

August frowned. "I had to."

His lawyer gazed at him for a while, then placed her hand on top of his.

The case was quick. The twins sold them up the river.

"No one was supposed to get hurt," Roger said, pleading with August to understand. "Not even you."

Jack's hands shook the whole time.

Sixteen months in the psychiatric ward for them both, with the stipulation that they be kept away from each other. Separate facilities, then.

Jack looked terrified as they dragged him away. Too scared to even reach out for him or call his name.

GUT

They dressed him in a special orange uniform and escorted him down the hall to his room. The other patients shrank away from them and muttered fearfully at the large security officers that flanked August. He had never felt more anxious in his entire life. He tripped over his feet. One of the officers grabbed his arm in a crushing grip, jerking him upright. When they finally got to his room, the orderly said something that he couldn't hear over the roaring of his own blood. Then they slammed the door shut and left him in the dark.

August stood still where they had placed him in the middle of the room and clenched his hands into fists. He glanced at his roommate, who had scrambled as far away from him as he could without melting completely into the wall.

August gritted his teeth.

He had failed. He had failed in every possible way with every possible choice he had ever made. Jack was still crazy. He was alone. And he was in a prison of his own design. The embarrassment and regret were choking him from the inside out, and all of a sudden he was screaming.

It started small, but it bubbled bigger every minute. Rising black and ugly through the veins in his feet, up and up, bursting his cells and filling his lungs, encasing itself around his bones and finally spilling from his eyes, tacky like tar. It tumbled from his mouth in a howl of rage so deep it shook his teeth. The hairs rose on the back of his neck.

It was a shout of pain so pure and hot, he could have sworn it was burning out his eyes.

And then, like a living nightmare, his howl roused the other patients to noisemaking. Like a battle cry. It soared above the symphony of their screams of confusion and fear, the banging on the doors and the weeping. Soared above all. A phoenix that burned and fell to ash before it could set alight the room at the very end of the hall where the dreammaker lived, imprisoned by his visions. Unanchored and unnoticed in the dark.

LIKE MOST TERRIBLE THINGS

He got used to it.

Time passed both quickly and slowly in the hospital—kind of like a weird, oppressive summer vacation. Where every day seemed like it took ten thousand years, but then you looked up and three months had passed in what felt like an instant. They didn't expect much from him other than to get up and go through the sched-uled routine. After the first couple of weeks, his roommate had stopped flinching every time he walked into the room.

It wasn't difficult there. Of course, on the other hand, there was nothing to distract him from thinking about what had happened.

And if he thought about it too much, it got hard to breathe. But he couldn't not think about it because this was the first time in about ten years that Jack wasn't immediately accessible to him in some way. It felt . . . indescribably terrible. Like someone had chopped off his arm, or blinded him in one eye.

But as with most things, he got used to it. He didn't have a choice.

THE HOSPITAL

The thing that really killed him about being there was the tedium. Other than going to the library, writing, and sleeping, there wasn't much else to do. It's not like he could really make friends. August had had enough of dealing with crazy people to last him a lifetime.

Solitude was boring, but at least he didn't have to actively participate in his roommate's frantic ranting or enraged howling.

Besides that, the food was crap. Things were soggy, salty, bland, or had a mysterious texture. He was pretty sure everything had a mild sedative in it, and out of suspicion, he had tried not to eat for the first three weeks. But all that had gotten him was some more one-on-one therapy.

Sometimes when he went to bed, the only thing that could get him to sleep was thinking, *At least this isn't jail, at least this isn't jail,* over and over until he succumbed to exhaustion.

WISH

August sighed and slumped against the window. They wouldn't let anyone outside.

It was raining and some of the patients were afraid of the noise or got too excited. It was easier to just keep them all in, rather than having to keep track of who was allowed out and who wasn't. That was the thing about this place. It was so batshit that if you didn't have problems coming in, you'd definitely have them going out. But that was such a cliché that he never actually vocalized the thought.

He wanted to see Jack.

He wished they had been kind enough to jail them together. Let them be with each other. Let him stand at Jack's side, like he was meant to.

There was a wild animal inside him that wanted to claw at Jack's cell till his fingers bled, and to scream until Jack heard how much he didn't want to stay away. But he pushed the urge down and away.

Because he was sane. And he didn't belong here.

A PSYCHOLOGIST

"What were you thinking before your actions on January thirtieth?"

August closed his eyes. He didn't remember thinking any-thing. It had been too far past the point where he'd simply decided to stop thinking altogether.

"You have to answer the questions, Mr. Bateman. It is a part of your treatment."

His psychologist changed every other month or so. This month's version was stern, bearded, and encased in tweed.

"It wasn't so much thinking," August said after some time. "It was more like following instructions. And for the record, I swear I've told you guys this before. Jack would ask me to do something and I would just do it. The concept isn't confusing."

"So, what you're saying is that everything is Mr. Rossi's fault."

"No. That's not what I said at all. It was definitely a two-person activity. There was just . . . obligation involved. It's really difficult to explain. Is what Jack said about it on file?"

"I'm sorry, but that's confidential information."

August propped his legs up on the desk in front of him defi-antly and crossed his arms. "Well, *I'm* sorry that you're such a dick."

STERILE

Hospital staff found him leaning against Jack's door with his hand splayed out over the small window. He'd thought that they would be put in separate facilities, but every day he woke up here, he felt otherwise. He decided to look. It had taken weeks, but he'd finally found it; August could feel him living behind the door. Sleeping, maybe. It was a warm March afternoon. It was very exciting.

"You're not allowed on this side of the hospital."

August whipped around angrily, getting ready to argue.

Oh. It was just the kind orderly. The one with the soft hands and the soft voice. "Let's get you back to your room."

August let her lead him down the hall and down the stairs and through the corridor. She was gentle as she brought him to bed and tucked him inside, pulling the covers up to his chin. Before he fell asleep, he felt her hand brush over his hair.

"You poor thing."

GINGHAM

The kind orderly was back. August sat up in his bed. She didn't come with security, and she closed his room door gently behind her, and sat down at the foot of his bed. "I know I shouldn't be doing this, but it's very hard to watch from the outside and not want to help. I went to Mr. Rossi's room today. He spoke about you."

"Does he know I'm here?" August asked calmly.

She wrung her hands in her lap. "He . . . hasn't been getting better. He has moments of lucidity, but most of the time he's just . . . Anyway, he spoke about you. He asked for you. Quite rudely, I might add."

August laughed fondly. "Yeah, yeah. He's like that."

They sat in silence. August picked at his sheets self-consciously. "Do you think you could . . . I don't know . . . keep doing this for us? It's important."

After a moment, she nodded.

EIGHT MONTHS

The weather was nice, so they were allowed out today. The grass was crunchy and cold, but August lay down in it anyway. He closed his eyes and threaded his fingers through it, flinching as the frost turned to dew against his skin.

"You're weird. You don't belong here."

August cracked his eyes open against the glare of the sun. "May I help you?"

The girl had tightly braided pigtails and was swathed in a pink bathrobe. "He screams about you at night. The boy they keep in that little room. He's crazy. He's crazy. He's crazy." Her face looked pinched and mean.

August covered his face with his arm. "Please, go away."

She leaned over him. Her breath smelled like medicine and decay. "Poor little boy in his cage. Poor useless knight. You never come when he calls."

August took his arm down and just stared at her. Stared at her because he knew she didn't like to be looked at.

"Stop it! Stop it!" she shrieked. "You're just jealous! You're just jealous of me!"

He stared at her until the orderlies dragged her away.

PILLS

The orderlies followed him everywhere now.

He took his medicine now.

He slept for days.

It was like languishing in a cottony haze: cotton over his eyes, cotton in his ears, cotton in his mind. It was easier to take his medicine than to think about Jack trapped in his room less than five hundred feet away. It might as well have been miles.

Codependency, they called it.

co·de·pen·dent

[koh-di-pen-duhnt]

adjective:

1. *Of, or pertaining to, a relationship in which one person is physically or psychologically addicted, as to alcohol or gambling, and the other person is psychologically dependent on the first in an unhealthy way.*

"Does that sound familiar?" the psychologist asked him. His shrink was a young man this time.

August laughed. "Yeah. Yeah, it does. What are you going to do about it? I like it just the way it is. What are you going to do?"

MOMENTUM

"You're a smart boy, August," the psychologist said. The doctor was young. Pretty, this time. Probably Korean. She wore her glasses on the edge of her nose and smiled at him often. "The difficulty with this case is your reluctance to advance with your therapy. From what I've heard from my colleagues, you reach near breakthrough, then stop opening up and instead make flippant remarks until they're forced to end the session with you. I don't think it's that you don't understand. I think you're acting out on purpose so you can stay near Mr. Rossi."

August shrugged, but inside he was impressed. It had been six months and she was the only one who had noticed.

The psychologist began writing something on her notepad. "Unlike others who have handled your case, I think that you would benefit from *less* separation from Mr. Rossi, because it is not having the intended effect. At this point it just seems to be exacerbating your codependency. It is, however, a part of the conditions of your sentence, so I can't do much about it. I can, however, make arrangements to increase your likelihood of seeing him." She stopped writing and looked at him hard. "In order to do so I need your cooperation. I need you to trust me and I need you to stop acting out. We need to have confidentiality because I will be doing things that could put me at risk, not to mention complicate your case. You have eight months left and a parole hearing coming up in four weeks. Is this something you want, August? Because it's the only way I see that can accelerate your therapy."

"Yes." He didn't wait a second to think about it. It was worth it.

The psychologist tore a small scrap of paper from her notepad. "My cell phone number."

He folded the paper until it was very small, then tucked it in the waistband of his pants.

Morton Rehabilitation
Therapy Center

Psychologist Treatment Plan

Case Number: 5320   Date of Session: 10/20/03
Client Name: August Bateman   Time of Session: 2:30
Individuals at Session: _____

Individual Session ☒   Group Session ☐   Family Session ☐   No Show ☐

Patient's Progress: First session assessment — Advanced Separation Anxiety, Mild depression, maybe PTSD.

Goal(s) addressed during session: Figure out why previous sessions were ineffective. Make breakthrough with patient.

Treatment dynamics and treatment intervention: Patient expresses growing anxiety about the weakening bond between him and his accomplice, fellow patient Jack Rossi. He finds any intervention to be a personal attack on the emotional safe space he has created for himself and Mr. Rossi.

Focus for next treatment session: Gain trust

Medications: Antidepressants

Doctor Name: Kimberly Cho   Date: 10/20/03
Signature: Ko Kim. Cho

AVE MARIA

The psychologist pulled him to the side during mealtime. "He gave me something to give to you. I read it and it didn't make much sense."

"That's okay. Give it to me." August snatched the paper out of her hand and opened it. His heart raced at the sight of Jack's spindly handwriting.

> The morning sun rose pink and gold above the field
> and, oh glorious Ives, how his armor shimmered in the light.
> How the feathers on his helmet framed his face. This is what
>   had been missing all along.
> And as the champion stood, boots firm on the ground,
>   howling to the sky, I knew at once that he'd never been
>   mine at all.
> He was a thing of the earth. He belonged to the streams
>   and the deserts and the darkness. To the sound of thunder
>   and the whispers of the ocean as it clawed the shore. To the
>   rain that fell when the sun was still blazing, to the grime
>   clenched between my fingers.
> I stood at his side.
> Nothing but the king of a kingdom of mud. But I threw my
>   head back anyway and joined his cry.
> They send word on the wing of a bird
> but faces are my currency,

and till i'm paid in full, they may as well send nothing.
    11:23 2:45

August flushed. It was *obscene*.

"What does it mean?"

"He just . . . misses me. Thank you for this. I . . . really appreciate it."

The psychologist nodded, but looked as if she didn't quite believe him. August smiled to reassure her and tucked the note in his waistband to keep it for later.

"You should smile more often," she tossed over her shoulder as she walked down the hall. "It's a good look on you."

CHLORPROMAZINE

He didn't even see him. He *felt* him first. Felt the weight of his gaze on the back of his neck. August turned around and there he was— walking between two orderlies. Thinner and frailer than August had ever seen him. Cheekbones jutting out, white and wan. But his eyes. They *burned*.

He heard the orderlies crying out for security before his fingers even touched Jack's hospital gown. "Jack. *Jack!*" He buried his face in Jack's neck and clung to him, frantically trying to memorize the feel of him, the *smell* of him.

"My Champion."

August sobbed.

"August, you have to let go. You have to do it on your own," Jack murmured against the soft curve of August's ear. August lurched backward from Jack instantly, like Jack was made of acid. The guards thundered down the hallway like a storm on the horizon.

"Are you okay?" August asked weakly. He still wanted to touch Jack so bad. He wanted Jack's clawlike fingers back on the nape of his neck. He wanted it to hurt so he could still feel it later. He wanted it so bad he could hardly breathe. He reached out again.

The guards tackled him to the floor.

Morton Rehabilitation Therapy Center

INCIDENT REPORT

Name: Janet Woolworth   Title: Charge Nurse

Unit: Juvenile Psychiatric ward   Phone Number: ext 5378

Involvement in incident: Witnessed incident and directed intervention

Signature: _____   Date: 10/28/03

INFORMATION ON INCIDENT

Date of incident: 10/28/03   Time of incident: 10:07 AM

Nature of incident: Physical outburst   Location of incident: Nurses' Station

Patients involved in incident: August Bateman, Jack Rossi

Staff involved: N. January Lee, PA. Stan Reeves

Staff in charge at time of incident: Nurse Janet Woolworth

Description of incident: High-security patient August Bateman came into contact with high-security patient Jack Rossi at the Nurses' Station. He handled Mr. Rossi roughly and needed to be restrained by security. Once the two patients were disengaged and Mr. Rossi was removed from the location, Mr. Bateman become compliant.

No injuries were sustained by either party. However, the unauthorized contact between the two patients is a direct violation of Mr. Bateman's court-ordered restrictions. Mild punitive action was taken.

COMPLETE ONLY IF NEEDED POLICE INTERVENTION

Police Station Name, Number: _____

Responding Officer(s): _____

Address of Station: _____ Phone: _____

HALVED AND BOUND

"Did you like your gift?"

August scrunched up his nose. "What are you talking about?"

"Jack. In the hallway. I arranged to see him so he would be moved from his room when pills are dealt out, about the time when your name should have been called. The two of you should have crossed paths, if I planned it correctly? I apologize for any resulting punishment."

"No . . . no . . . that was fine . . . *You* did that?"

"Yes," the psychologist said calmly. "What did you feel when you saw him?"

August paused. Then, deciding she had more than earned his honesty, he answered. "Desperation, mostly. Panic. And beneath that, relief and worry."

"What were you desperate for?" she asked, quickly jotting down his response.

August blushed. "A lot of things. I was desperate to be alone with him, so the orderlies and other patients would stop staring at us. Desperate for time to talk to him. I felt like I wanted to simultaneously . . . crawl inside his skin and pull him so close that we fused together." He laughed with embarrassment. "It's gross, I know."

"It's not gross," she said kindly. "May I ask you something else?" He waited. "Had you ever felt like that before your stay here?"

"No . . . not like that. It was never like that."

FEALTY

August had studied the verse Jack sent to him. He'd kept it well hidden, folded small. At first he'd wanted to carry it with him, like a talisman, but that seemed far too risky. So instead, he hid it in the gap between the molding and the wall.

11:23 2:45

It was a date and time. It was written so it couldn't be deciphered at passing glance. The only thing that tipped him off was the 45. It could have been two different times, but that would be useless, so it had to be a date and a time. And there aren't forty-five days in a month, so 2:45 had to be the time and 11:23 had to be the date.

That gave him hope. Jack was speaking in code. That took effort, so August knew Jack's mind couldn't have rotted completely away if he was still doing that.

Tonight was November 23, fifteen minutes from 2:45 a.m.

August got up from bed and pulled the string he'd used to rig the lock to his room, and the door unlocked with a soft click. He opened the door and stepped into the hall.

DORMOUSE

Jack cracked his door open a bit and gestured for August to come in. August glanced around. Then he walked quickly, slipping silently into Jack's room. They both closed the door as slowly as possible, then leaned against it, staring at each other. Alone.

Jack's eyes were very gray as he studied him, and August shrank beneath the other boy's gaze. "You look tired," Jack said.

"You look near dead," August replied.

Jack's laughter was hollow. He ran a skeletal hand through his hair and looked upset. August had never seen Jack's hair before. It had always been shorn so short that you couldn't quite tell what color it was. It was blond and brittle, like he hadn't had water in years.

"I don't know what to say now," August admitted. Every molecule in August's body was hungry and demanding. But he couldn't just take what he wanted. That wasn't how this worked. He needed permission.

"Wow. You're, like, *shaking*. And I can still see you as you! I didn't expect that. Everything else is just—" Jack waved his hand around to describe the crazy, and August tracked the movement with his eyes.

It got quiet again. August gathered his courage and reached out. Then he paused.

Jack smiled and it cut him to the core.

PULP

August gasped as Jack pulled his hair fiercely. "We don't have much time. They'll find you soon," he said.

August was barely listening. He scrambled to get closer, pulling up the back of Jack's shirt so he could brush his thumb against the crosshatch on Jack's ribs. The wicker that he'd unwittingly etched into Jack's skin.

"I miss the way you fucking smell," Jack admitted, his voice thick. August hummed his agreement into Jack's chest as he curled close to him.

"Christ, you're completely mad."

"I don't care. You're the most precious thing in the world to me. They're trying to make you forget that. *Don't let them make you forget it.*" August sighed.

It hurt to say. Like someone had reached down his throat, pulled his organs out through his mouth, and deposited them in Jack's lap.

"*August.*" With a single word, the Wicker King accepted his sentiment and wore it proudly.

"I can hear them looking for me," August whispered.

"We didn't have enough time. This isn't enough."

"Will it ever be?"

"They're coming down the hall. They'll be here soon." Jack

pulled him so hard, so close, that his bones protested, but his heart? It sang, keening at the feeling.

Then they drew back, stepping out from under the ropes of obligation and sentiment. The Wicker King and his Champion sat next to each other on Jack's bed. Close, but not touching. And waited for the guards to open the door.

INCIDENT REPORT

Morton Rehabilitation Therapy Center

INFORMATION ON PERSON REPORTING INCIDENT

Name: Susan Mohlmann   Title: Head Nurse

Unit: Juvenile Psychiatric ward   Phone Number: ext 5147

Involvement in incident: Reported to after incident happened

Signature: _____   Date: 11/23/03

INFORMATION ON INCIDENT

Date of incident: 11/23/03   Time of incident: 02:50 AM

Nature of incident: Violating restrictions   Location of incident: Patient's room

Patients involved in incident: August Bateman, Jack Rossi

Staff involved: N. January Lee, PA. Jessica Stone

Staff in charge at time of incident: Nurse Susan Mohlmann

Description of incident: High-security patient August Bateman was found in the hospital room of high-security patient Jack Rossi after hours. There was no evidence of a physical altercation. This is the second time Mr. Bateman has broken his court-ordered restriction.
Due to Mr. Bateman's inability to follow his restraining order, he has been secluded to his room for upwards of 3 weeks.

COMPLETE ONLY IF NEEDED POLICE INTERVENTION

Police Station Name, Number: _____

Responding Officer(s): _____

Address of Station: _____   Phone: _____

"WHY?" August shouted, pushing away from the table and standing up. "Why do I have to always be the responsible one?"

The psychologist raised an eyebrow at him. "Well, mostly because you're not actually dealing with a serious mental illness. You're a bit obsessive, codependent, and clearly possess a terrible sense of judgment. But regardless of what happened at court, you're not criminally insane. Jack? Jack is actually ill. Instead of letting him lead you, why don't you step up and lead him?"

August sat back down. He put his head in his hands. "I don't want to," he said quietly.

"Excuse me? I didn't hear you."

"I don't *want* to," August said a little louder. "I *like* following him. Following orders. Doing whatever he wants. It feels good. It feels so fucking good."

"Why do you think that is?"

"I just . . . I know what to do with myself when he tells me what

277

to do. He's my king. When you lock him away from me, lock me away from him—it hurts us. It hurts *me*." August was crying now. He couldn't stop.

"You need to calm down."

"No! I'm finished fucking being calm. I've been explaining this for months. No one ever fucking listens! I have never known a time when he wasn't there to lead. That's why I burned down the toy factory. That is why I let him practically drown me. Because it was worth it. It's so fucking simple. Why can't any of you get it into your fucking heads: He is my only constant. My fixed point."

". . . they found out that he had a tumor."

"Wait, what?" He couldn't quite hear over the roaring in his ears.

"Jack had a tumor pressing on a section of his brain," the psychologist said slowly. "Six more weeks and the damage would have been irreparable. The hallucinations weren't the illness itself. They were only a symptom, and as the tumor grew, the symptom shifted as well—hence, the progressive darkening of his vision from pleasant images to threatening and terrifying delusions. His condition is called peduncular hallucinosis. It's rare, but thankfully it's curable. He's having the tumor removed next week."

August stared at the floor. He clenched his hands into fists.

"You couldn't have known."

He laughed mirthlessly at that. "I always tried to do my best by him . . . ," August whispered.

The psychologist looked tired. "There was nothing you could have done—"

"Don't. Patronize me," August spat, looking up at her. "I could have taken him to a *hospital*, called his *mom*, talked to the *school*. Hell, I had the opportunity to get him to a psychologist for free. But I didn't do any of that. I indulged him and I wasted time."

"August—"

"No. We aren't talking about this. I can't talk about this right now. Take me back to my room."

"If you would just—"

August got up silently, picked up his chair, and hurled it against the wall with astonishing violence. The wood splintered with a loud crack. "TAKE ME BACK."

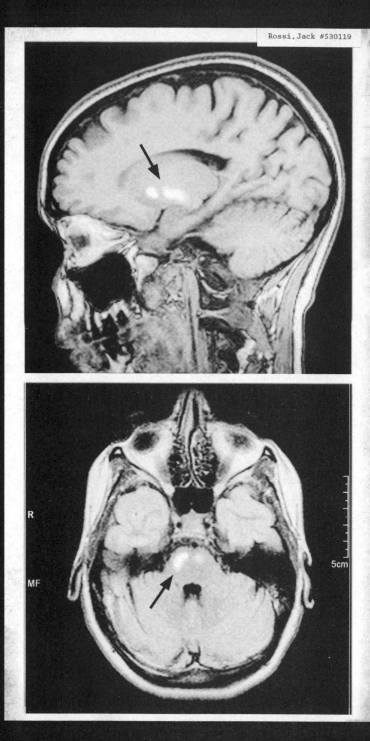

Morton Rehabilitation
Therapy Center

Patient Observation Chart

Name: Rossi, Jack

Patient No.: 530119

DOB: 03/18/85

Admitted Date 02/07/03 Ward Juv. Psy.

Transferred Date _____ Ward _____

Transferred Date _____ Ward _____

Patient Observations

Assessment

Patient was admitted with complaints of visions and persistent
headaches. Psychological exam indicated fragmented sleep, day-
time hypersomnia, headaches, and hallucinations. After prelimi-
nary physical exam the following tests were run:

- MRI
- Urine analysis
- Electrocardiogram
- Complete blood count
- Complete metabolic panel
- Chest x-ray
- Thyroid function and toxicology
- Vitamin B-12 levels and thiamine

Impressions

The physical work up was negative with no focal neurological defi-
cits. Mental status and psychiatric evaluation showcased severe
anxiety, and habitual disassociation, presumed to be associated
with the trauma of delay reporting the illness. MRI shows intra-
cranial pathology pressing on the left cerebral peduncle, thus
confirming a diagnosis of peduncular hallucinosis. Surgical
intervention is highly recommended.

STAFF INFORMATION

Doctor/Nurse Pracitioner Name: Dr. Sophia Batca, M.D.

Date of assessment: 12/10/03

HOME

August barely ate the week Jack had surgery. He curled up into a ball of guilt on his bed, his eyes dry and prickly. He should have been finishing up senior year. Should have been laughing with Gordie and going to midterms and complaining about homework.

He missed his mom.

He missed real food, like lasagna and salmon and fresh vegetables.

He missed the woods and his fires and the look of thirst in Jack's eyes when he was on a bender.

He missed Rina, with her sweet mouth and beautiful mind.

He missed the sound of silence.

Everything here rattled or beeped or groaned or yelled or cried, and August was fucking sick of it.

PLANS

They left him alone for a while. As long as he got up to shower and eat something at least once a day, no one spoke to him or asked him to do anything. He even got out of group therapy for a week, which was a relief. But it wasn't sustainable. His case evaluation hearing was tomorrow.

August wasn't sure whether he was ecstatic at the chance to get out of here, terrified about what waited for him outside, or entirely too reluctant to leave Jack behind. It wasn't something he could handle while knowing that Jack was still recovering from brain surgery. And fuck if he would leave before saying good-bye.

Every day he asked the nice orderly when Jack was coming back, and every day she said she didn't know. She wasn't a higher-up, she was just an orderly; they didn't trust her with that information.

That was okay. He just needed to be here when it happened. It was too cruel to turn his back on this place with his king still trapped inside it.

GRIFTING

The hearing came. August sat quietly in his chair and listened while they described him as "gentle, protective, and under a lot of stress." Also, apparently codependency wasn't in the *DSM*-IV, so he couldn't be held for that alone.

It was decided that he would remain at the hospital for one more month for stabilization and rehabilitation purposes before his release, on the stipulation that he continue seeing his resident therapist for three more months.

There wasn't extensive property damage from the fire, outside of the abandoned building itself. But he would still be required to pay $2,000 in fines due to the closeness of the burn site to the nature preserve forest area, along with destruction of public property.

August went back to the ward with promises of significantly less restriction and a significant increase in privileges, but he really just wanted to sleep for days.

CHANSONNIER

The Raven

The Golden Bird

The Eagle of the North

The Champion with Sparks in His Veins

The King's Lionheart

The Bringer of the Blue

Defender of Light

Would it still be real after the treatment, or would all his titles collapse like a tower of sand?

Would Jack look at him from across a table years from now and see the hero of this story? Or would he just see a man? A friend?

Nothing so glorious as to be shouted from the rooftops or cemented in legend.

Or was "friend" enough of a title to satisfy? After all of this?

August didn't know. And it kept him up at night.

BIND AND BREAK AND FIND AND TAKE

They brought Jack back at night, when they knew August would be sleeping. August was banned from the entire left wing of the institution, where the more fragile patients were kept, for three full days while Jack recovered and readjusted to life without his vision clouded by hallucinations.

The nice orderly had been coming into his room every so often to bring news. Today she came in and shut the door behind her. August sat up in bed. "He asked me to tell you that he's being acquitted as a condition of him going through with the surgery. It's likely that he'll have to pay fines, but otherwise, he should be released."

"When is he leaving?" August asked.

"As soon as possible. He'll likely be gone before you. I overheard one of the doctors in the hallway talking with the director. He said that he'd only be here for a couple more days. It's likely that the only reason he didn't go straight home after the week of recovering from his surgery is because they can't release him from the hospital before first settling things here in the ward."

August began getting up. "I need to see him."

She put a hand on his shoulder. "You need to stay here. You're so close to getting out, August. You can't do anything to jeopardize that. You have a month left. Don't make it six more. You and I both know that it's not worth it."

"Okay, yeah . . . okay." August went to lie back down, like a titan finally falling to dust.

CIRRUS

He was dreaming. He had to be, because he was walking through the hospital in broad daylight. No one stopped him. No one told him to go back to his room. There were no guards. There was just the sun coming through the windows and the unbearable stifling white, washed golden in the light.

He walked the length of the hospital to the room he was forbidden from entering and opened the door. There was nothing inside. August searched the room. Then, disappointed, he went out into the hallway.

"He's not there. He was never there."

An orderly he had never seen before stood at the end of the hallway.

"What do you mean, he was never there? Of course he was there! Just because nobody is in there now doesn't mean no one was ever there at all," August said, frustrated.

August turned to gesture back at the empty room, but found it wasn't empty at all.

Jack sat on the bed. He knew it was him by the way he curled one leg gracefully under the other, but his entire head was obscured by a large white cloud. August stumbled into the room and fell to his knees. As soon as they hit the tile, they were no longer covered by rough cloth, but clad in the finest steel.

"Are you certain, Lionheart?" The orderly was in the doorway now.

"Of course," August said, bowing before him. "I never doubted once."

When he looked up, the room was empty and the armor was gone and the orderly had vanished.

When August woke up, he wept.

OKAY

"I feel as though your stay here has been less than advantageous for you," the psychologist said.

"What makes you think that?" August replied. He took a bite of his apple, pilfered at lunch.

"If I was to be completely honest, you're much worse now than when you came in. The only thing we seem to have fixed is your pyromania."

August snorted. He wasn't a pyromaniac. He hadn't had the urge since he'd nearly burned off the entire first layer of skin on his palms. Which was totally a rational response. If they wanted to take credit for that, whatever.

"It's likely that Jack will come out of this situation with significantly less trauma than you will," the psychologist remarked. "The procedure is invasive, but the recovery time for this illness is notoriously very short. Only a couple of days, actually. If the surgery is successful, he should be right as rain."

August took another bite.

"How do you feel about that?"

He chewed for a bit instead of answering.

"What's your name? You know, I never asked. Or cared to find out, before now," he said suddenly.

"Kimberly Cho."

"Dr. Cho?"

"Yes?"

"Thanks. You know. For everything."

Morton Rehabilitation Therapy Center

Psychologist Treatment Plan

Case Number: _53120_
Client Name: _August Bateman_
Individuals at Session: _____

Date of Session: _12/22/03_
Time of Session: _2:30_

Individual Session ☒ Group Session ☐ Family Session ☐ No Show ☐

Patient's Progress: _____

Goal(s) addressed during session: _Preparation for release_

Treatment dynamics and treatment intervention: _Patient says he is sluggish and tired, but he seems happy. He is compliant with the medication and therapy requirements conditional to his release._

Focus for next treament session: _____

Medications: _Renewed previous prescriptions._

Doctor Name: _Kimberly Cho_   Date: _12/22/03_
Signature: _Kim Cho_

It was night when he came. The guard turned on the light and searched the room before waving him in. August sat up in bed and watched the guard close the door behind him. He could see the man still looking in through the tiny window. Ah well, it couldn't be helped. August turned his attention to Jack.

Jack stood awkwardly in the middle of the room. He was wearing regular clothes and his head was shaved because of the surgery. He looked pretty much like he had the day they'd arrived. Maybe a bit thinner and a bit paler, but no worse for wear.

"Can I?" Jack gestured at the bed. August nodded.

Jack approached him hesitantly and sat on the edge. "I'm leaving tomorrow," he blurted out. "I wanted to see you before I did."

August cleared his throat. "So the surgery . . . the surgery worked, huh?"

"Yup." Jack picked at the sheets for a bit before continuing. "It's weird, you know? I wouldn't say I miss it, but it's weird. It's a good thing it's over, though, I guess. Or at least that's what they keep telling me."

"Is it permanent?" August asked, his voice cracking.

"Yeah. Yes it is."

August felt a lump rising in his throat and he didn't know why. He turned away from Jack and glared at the barred window.

ALLEGRETTO

"Are you . . . mad at me?"

August shook his head, but he gripped the edge of the blanket tighter. When he turned back, Jack was visibly upset.

"No, I'm not mad at you, Jack, I could never be . . . I am angry, though. I think I've been angry since it began . . . I'm angry that we have nothing to show for it. I'm angry that we couldn't fix you on our own. I'm angry that I'm still here and you're going to leave me here—" August bit his tongue at the pain of that thought, and closed his eyes.

When he opened them, Jack was frowning very hard.

August shook his head and forced a smile. "But that's not important. I'm glad you're not sick anymore. Do you think they'll let you back on the team?"

"I don't care about the team, August. Why are you even . . . August? August, look at me. *Look at me*."

He couldn't. "It was nice to see you, Jack, but I think you should go," he said.

"No!" Jack scrambled closer, but August didn't react. "No, please! I'm sorry, August. I'm sorry."

August just stared at the floor.

"I'm sorry." Jack was crying now. Everything in August was screaming at him to do something—he always did something when Jack cried. But instead, he just sat there and said:

"I'm always going to *be* a part of this world that doesn't even exist anymore. I'm always going to look at you and . . ." August paused. "At one point it was just a game. At the river it was supposed to be a game. But now I can't stop. I never could. I'm always going to want to be at your heels, fighting for you. Hurting myself because you tell me to. It's fucked up and I'm fucked up now, too."

Jack's face constricted with pain. He gripped August's shoulders and shook him.

"I never said I didn't feel the same," Jack said harshly. "Just because I don't see the kingdom doesn't mean it doesn't still exist," Jack said furiously. "As long as one of us remembers it, it still counts. We decide the end of the game, not them. Not anyone else. You're so stupid, August. You're so stupid and I love you so much."

MODERATO

"I love you and we don't need the other world to keep that." He glanced at the small window in the door to see if the guard was watching, then leaned over quickly and pressed their foreheads together.

"It's just true," he said. "It always has been. In this world and the next. They could take everything away and leave us with nothing, and I would still love you."

Jack's face went blurry, like August was seeing it through the sea.

"Do they still sing songs of my victory?" August choked.

"They do. And they'll crescendo like beacons to the farthest reaches. With every new breath of life that forms in a world without darkness that came at the price of your hands and your mind."

"You've become a poet," August breathed.

"I haven't." Jack laughed softly. "I'm just telling you what I saw carved into the walls before they stole that world from me. You were chosen as *Champion*, August. Not a martyr."

Jack brushed the salt from August's cheek.

"I've never seen you cry before," he whispered.

Then, with a resolute and terrible sorrow, Jack cradled August's cheek in his nervously shaking hands and kissed him.

GLORY

August's heart seized.

He didn't . . . know he could have this.

Jack kissed him so carefully that August thought he would fall to pieces. Kissed him with the weight of knowing the price of risk. Then he gazed back at August like his heart was already breaking.

It was the same face that Jack had made on the roof, in the middle of the night, when they rolled in the grass, when he sat back with August's blood and ink on his hands, when his face was lit orange with flames, when he'd opened the door to Rina's room, when he stared across the gym at the homecoming dance, when he pulled him from the river and breathed him back to life.

Jack had been waiting. He'd been trying. He was scared. There were tears in his eyes and it took August's breath away.

They were being watched, but August didn't care. He curled his fingers into Jack's shirt and dragged him closer.

"How long?" He had to know.

"August, please—"

"How long have you been waiting for me?" The words tore themselves roughly from his throat.

Jack closed his eyes and hung his head in despair. It had been before all of this, then. Maybe even earlier.

August brushed his fingertips against the sharp edge of Jack's jaw. Then he touched the edge of the bandage on the side of Jack's head.

"I'm right here," he said. "I've always been right here."

The sound Jack made was so quiet and so desperately lonely. So August closed the last inch between them, and answered it. He ate up the noises Jack made, sweet and lush as they were, and tasted the rest of their lives.

"When we are free and have healed from this, will you stay?" he gasped. "Will you stay with me?"

The guard pounded on the door. Jack jerked back from him with a start and placed his hands in full view of the window. He was still wrecked and wanting, glorious and raw. August reached back out for him, instinctively, but Jack shook his head, scrambling to his feet as the door began to open.

"I have to go. But I'll be back for you," Jack promised.

"Mr. Rossi, your time is up."

"I'll be back for you. I always will."

The door shut loudly behind him, and August was once again left alone in the dark.

WHITE

He had three weeks left to spend alone in the ward. Some days passed quickly. Others stretched into years. Every movement was weighed down by a thousand pounds of lethargy.

How can you breathe with hands squeezing your lungs, or see when your sun has been struck from the sky?

Sometimes August walked the hallways. Technically, he didn't have to stay in his room anymore, so he went around looking at everything, trying to put the whole experience to memory. They allowed him to have paper now, and he'd stolen a pen from Dr. Cho's office, so sometimes he even wrote. He wasn't very good at it yet, but one day he would be better.

Maybe he would skip over this part and just write the story of the adventure. Like a children's book. Concentrate on the mystery and magic and leave out the fire, hunger, and fear. They could keep that for themselves. Whisper of it in the dark, fifty years from now, over whiskey and expensive cigars.

It would just be another one of those small hardships packaged away and sent to where history goes to die. Leaving the tale as untouched and lovely as the fall morning when they'd first found the toy factory.

Boarded up and whole.

POST

They gave him his letters at the end. They'd held them from him all this time.

One was from Roger, the other was a padded envelope from Rina. He opened Roger's first:

Dear August,

Peter said you wouldn't want to hear from us. He's probably right, but I didn't want you to think we were mad at you or forgot about you. I know we can get a little bit . . . I don't know. But Peter cares, even if he acts like he's too smart or strong to.

Anyway, after you left they boarded up the factory for good. Peter and I stopped by to see. They put up a "for lease" sign and everything. It was the only thing anyone talked about for weeks after you left. Kids had been going over there and acting like it's haunted. I'm glad they boarded it up. I didn't think you'd like that.

Everyone else is doing all right. Gordie got into Yale, which surprised everyone. Peter and I are going to Brown and Alex decided to stay in town and get a job in the town next to us. She told us to tell you that she'll make you as many muffins as you like when you get back.

I don't know if they let you send letters in there, but if they do, can you send one back?

Your friend,

Roger

August folded it back up and pulled out Rina's.

It was a page ripped out of a notebook with a bit of lipstick smeared messily at the corner and some speckles of coffee on the sides. Crammed inside was a single tea bag of that dark spiced tea she always drank.

Jack came back to me.

I got a new apartment where the carpet is softer and the streetlights don't shine through the windows at night.

Come home.

PLEASE, LET ME GET WHAT I WANT

"Returned to you is one backpack, which had in it one sweater, three rags, a lighter, a cell phone, a notebook, ten pencils, a wallet with two bus cards and $35.03 inside it. And here are your street clothes. You can change in the bathroom inside the ward, but must remain inside the lobby once your uniform has been removed. You can bring it to the front desk."

August shucked off his hospital pants and put his legs back into the jeans he'd been wearing when he'd arrived. The cloth felt rough in comparison, and it still smelled of ash and fire. It was much more comfortable to finally be dressed like himself, though.

"Good-bye, August. Best of luck!"

He politely waved back at the orderly. He didn't know her, but the well-wishes were appreciated.

August rummaged around in his backpack for his cell phone and turned it on. He quickly dialed his home number and waited for his mom to pick up. He expected the answering machine. He hung up and quickly dialed Jack, but the line was busy.

August flipped his phone closed and sat in one of the cushioned lobby chairs. He pulled his knees up to his chin and hid his face in his arms. Maybe he should just walk home. His mom was probably there, sitting in the basement watching game shows like he'd never left.

FORTENTOOK

August gasped and looked up into the light. He'd almost dozed off, but then was jolted awake by a hand in his hair. It brushed through gently once or twice, then tightened without warning and roughly pulled his head back.

The Wicker King leaned down and pressed their foreheads together.

The noise August made was violent in its relief. He surged up and clung to him like a man to a mast in the eye of a storm. Jack laughed in surprise, and then made soft hushing sounds, grounding him with the sharp pain of his grip.

"Through doom and dust," Jack recited.

"You *came back*," August whispered, like it was breaking his heart.

"I couldn't not. Do you have all your things?"

"I think so."

"Then come on. I'll take you home."

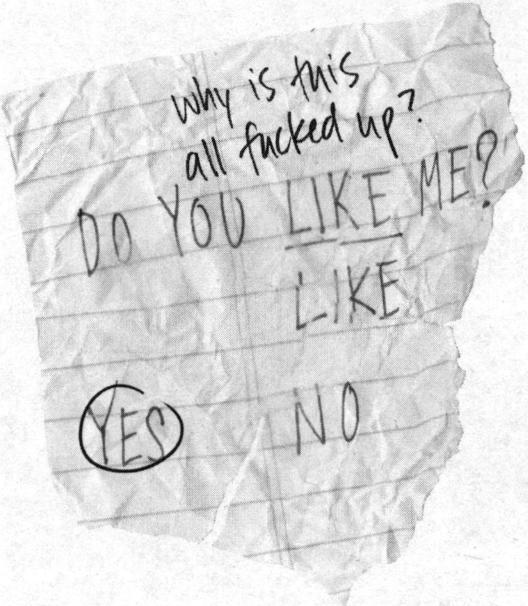
why is this
all fucked up?
DO YOU LIKE ME?
LIKE
YES
NO

August and Jack's legend continues in their fantasy world . . .

THE LEGEND OF THE GOLDEN RAVEN

Long ago, when the earth was still young, there were two kings: the King of the Wood and the Wicker King.

They were brothers and their kingdoms lay side by side, shuttered away behind a wall. The two kings were fair and just, mischievous and fond of sport. They were generous, brave, and well loved by their people. It was a golden age, when the fruit hung ever ripe from the trees and milk animals grew fat and plenty.

Every year in midsummer, when the second sun was highest in the sky, there was a Great Hunt. All the eligible men and women joined together to go out into the wildlands to capture a great beast for the midsummer feast.

But a black fog seethed and roiled outside the country wall. It was a wild, hungry thing made of sorcery that had been banished by the Champion and the capital council in the days of old, five hundred seasons past. It was held back from swallowing them all by the country's greatest boon, a living stone: the Rapturous Blue . . .

*Read more of this digital short, along with Jack's
version of the story, wherever ebooks are sold.*

NOTE FROM THE AUTHOR

When I was a bit closer to your age than I am now, something terrible happened.

Like August and Jack, I tried my best to fix it myself and learned many harsh lessons that I sincerely wish I hadn't. While this book is entirely fiction, the situations the main characters found themselves in may be all too real for some of us. I would be doing a disservice to you—and to the me that I was—if I did not address them.

Jack and August are both victims of neglect. They are neglected by their parents and ignored by all figures of authority around them until it is entirely too late. The structure of their relationship and the journey that they take are only the symptoms of this larger and more pressing issue.

Like most teenagers, Jack and August both need certain things in order to thrive. They need to care and feel cared for; they need structure and authority; they need unconditional support; they need someone to be concerned for them; they need to be able to rely on someone; and they need to feel safe. Because those things were absent in their lives, they tried to build versions of them within each other. Then, because they had no other options, they took these things from each other until they both had nothing left to give.

August needed to care for someone to feel like he had his life in control, so Jack made himself easy to care for. When August grew exhausted from caring too much, Jack took the reins of authority in the only way August would accept. When Jack needed unconditional support, August gave it happily. When Jack needed to feel safe, August made a home for Jack in his house—and in his own mind. They were always designed to be perfectly balanced. Like an ouroboros: eating while being eaten.

There were so many opportunities for figures of authority to disrupt that pattern. Their parents, who were never there. Teachers, who preferred to reprimand them for their uncharacteristic actions instead of being concerned. The dean, who was more interested in disrupting August's income instead of wondering why he needed it. The nurses and social workers their high school undoubtedly had, who were missing entirely from this narrative, having never been alerted to the problem. The police who took them to jail instead of to the hospital. August's lawyer, as well-meaning as she was. The only people who were not in some way at fault were all the young people in this story, who were doing the best they could with the situation they were given.

This is not uncommon. Many young people, perhaps like you, find themselves being forced to carry something they never imagined would be so heavy, with no one around to support them. It must be said that they are *rarely ever* at fault for the multitude of ways they choose to bear that load. Even if they are destructive. They are not "failing"; *someone has failed them.*

If you read this book and you see too much of your life in the codependence and neglect that is August's and Jack's lives, please know that it is not your fault.

If you are dealing with mental illness and you are exhausted, please know that it is not your fault.

If you are alone and overburdened, please know that it is not your fault.

Now, August and Jack are fictional. They wind up okay in the end. They'll learn how to love each other with fingertips, instead of claws. They will build a home and a life together, and there they will heal and grow.

You deserve to heal and grow, too. You deserve to have someone to talk to about your problem; you deserve unconditional support; you deserve care and safety and all the things you need to thrive. Just because you may not have them doesn't mean you don't deserve them. If someone tells you that you don't deserve those things, they are lying.

Keep trying your best.

Ask for help when you need it.

Do your best to be brave, but it is okay not to be.

If you drop the weight you're carrying, it is okay. You can build yourself back up out of the pieces.

If your mind stops listening to you, it's not your fault. There are billions of us; you are not alone.

And lastly, whoever you are:

I am so so proud of you.

Love,

Kayla

Additional Resources

http://www.crisischat.org/

http://www.crisistextline.org/ (mobile access)

National Youth Crisis Hotline: (800) 442-HOPE (4673)

Teen Help Adolescent Resources: (800) 840-5704

ACKNOWLEDGMENTS

I would like to thank thirteen-year-old Ryan M. for reading thirteen-year-old Kayla's self-insert, Mary Sue trash novellas while he should have been paying attention to class. Without you, I probably wouldn't have been brave enough to write anything better than that.

Thank you, Amy, Professor Bauer-Gatsos, Professor Simpson. Thank you, Imprint Team. And thanks, Mom and Dad, for letting me be me. That's a great and terrible thing, and I hope I'm worth it.

GOFISH

QUESTIONS FOR THE AUTHOR

K. ANCRUM

What did you want to be when you grew up?
I wanted to be a stylist, specifically for menswear. Even though
I've been writing since I was twelve, I've always loved textiles
and notions and the transformative power of style.

When did you realize you wanted to be a writer?
When people began reading my stories. I always wrote book-
length works, but I never really considered them to be of interest to anyone but myself until I began posting them on
tumblr and had people reach out to let me know that my work
emotionally impacted them. I was actually in school for fash-
ion merchandising and nearly finished, but switched to English
when I realized that being a writer was an achievable dream.

What's your most embarrassing childhood memory?
One day, when I was around sixteen, I heard the mailman
putting stuff in our mail receptacle. I had been waiting for a
package so I was really excited and got up to go empty it.
But apparently the mailman had only just paused to shuffle
through the mail and intended to put more in. So I opened
the slot on my side of the door and shoved my hand in at the
same time the mailman shoved his hand in and our hands

touched. He literally screamed and I snatched my hand out of the slot so fast. We both stood there on either side of the door, mutually re-living the horror for what seemed like a full two minutes: him, of touching a hand when he expected to feel mail; me because I nonconsensually touched a mailman and created this entire scenario with my impatience. Then, he turned and fast walked away from our house. He started leaving mail inside our screen door instead of the slot and it was 100% my fault.

What's your favorite childhood memory?

When I was about seven, I was obsessed with Laura Ingalls Wilder's Little House series. There was this scene in one of the books where the girls get an orange for Christmas, and the way they described it was utterly transcendent, because at the time oranges were such a rarity. So I told my mom that I wanted oranges for Christmas too. Instead of laughing or forgetting, she went out and bought me, like, eight different kinds of oranges months later, and I woke up to an orange bounty that Christmas. It was by far the loveliest and most thoughtful gift I've ever received.

As a young person, who did you look up to most?

My mom. She always tried very hard at things, even when it was something she wasn't naturally good at. Watching someone struggle and then succeed over and over again really framed my understanding of work ethic.

What was your favorite thing about school?

I always had really good solid groups of friends, who were funny, interesting and diverse. I really loved waking up every day to go see them.

What were your hobbies as a kid? What are your hobbies now?

It's unsurprising, but I loved to read and write. I would go through three or four books a day and would work on reading my short books during any free time I had all through middle school and deep into high school. I also loved painting and clay sculpture. Now, I read a lot of fan fiction. I'm very interested in media analysis and social participation in media.

Did you play sports as a kid?

I've played almost every sport and I hated them all. Unfortunately, I am exceptionally good at one thing that every sport requires while being hopelessly bad at all other features. It was seductive to the youth coaches, who relentlessly recruited me for things. But it was also unfailingly disappointing, which always gave me a viable escape route. For example, I'm good at physics and can make three-point shots in basketball with alarming accuracy, but I am very bad at dribbling. I can also run backward almost as fast as I can run forward, which is great for football, but I can't catch anything. Then, in spite of being unable to catch things, I'm exceptionally good at throwing things, which is great for baseball, but I can't hit things with a bat. I'm very fast, but only in bursts too short for competitive track. You see where this is going.

What was your first job, and what was your worst job?

My first job was a camp counselor and it was super fun! My worst job was a sales associate at a women's workwear store at a local mall. I still resent the coercive obligation to ask customers if they'll get one of our credit cards.

What book is on your nightstand now?
The Road to Little Dribbling by Bill Bryson

How did you celebrate publishing your first book?
I sat at home and frantically refreshed Amazon until it became available at midnight. And then I had a bit of a cry because it still felt so surreal.

Where do you write your books?
At work. I only write at home if I'm on a deadline and am binge-writing.

What challenges do you face in the writing process, and how do you overcome them?
I have ADHD and I procrastinate a lot. I don't allow that to destroy my life though, and work very hard to understand my own limitations (how many pages can I write in one night) and make sure that I meet any deadline that's given to me.

What is your favorite word?
Reluctant. It feels exactly like what it means as it rolls out of your mouth.

Who is your favorite fictional character?
Pippi Longstocking. She was unstoppable.

What was your favorite book when you were a kid? Do you have a favorite book now?
It was *The Giver* for many years, then *Ender's Game*. Now my favorite book is *I'm a Stranger Here Myself* by Bill Bryson. I really enjoy comedic writing and alternative perspectives.

SQUARE FISH

If you could travel in time, where would you go and what would you do?

I would probably go to the future. I'm incredibly interested in the potential for Solar Punk in post-capitalist Western society.

What's the best advice you have ever received about writing?

Someone once told me that I shouldn't care whether I'm a "good writer" and to focus on whether my audience enjoyed my writing. People can be so hard on themselves, but if their audience considers their work to be of consumable and enjoyable quality, that frustration is kind of unnecessary. Also, this same person told me to not worry about being a "perfect writer" because I'm young and will get better as I get older. Accepting that your current quality is **not** indicative of your ultimate potential makes accepting criticism easier. Because instead of letting it hurt you, it's easier to use it to help you grow.

What advice do you wish someone had given you when you were younger?

I wish someone had taught me to be even kinder. I wasn't a particularly cruel child, but looking back, I wish I had reached out to some kids I knew were struggling. We all have things we wished we hadn't said, and I'm not an exception to that.

Do you ever get writer's block? What do you do to get back on track?

I do! I use non-writing media to put me in a writing mood. For my newest book, *The Weight of the Stars*, I watched the film *Interstellar* almost ten times to put me in the mood. My writer's block is never about a lack of ideas and more about overriding the executive dysfunction that having ADHD comes with. Removing all distractions and hyper-focusing on media similar to the topic I'm writing about helps a lot.

What do you want readers to remember about your books?

I always write about teenagers who are trying. I think it's important to try, even if you don't succeed. I hope my readers see my characters trying and value their attempts as strongly as they should value their own attempts to try in their own lives.

What would you do if you ever stopped writing?

I think I would only ever stop writing because I was busy reading or consuming some other type of storytelling media. If I physically lost the ability to write traditionally, I would adapt and switch to speech-to-text applications. Creating and consuming stories is an integral part of life for me, and I absolutely must be doing one or the other.

If you were a superhero, what would your superpower be?

I would like to be able to grant one need-based wish for anyone and everyone I meet by warping the likelihood of probability. So, if the likelihood that they are accepted to their dream school is 1:100,000, I can touch them and change that likelihood to 1:2 at the most. That way I wouldn't be dramatically altering things in a way that would mess with the butterfly effect by altering isolated incidents, but instead by maximizing luck within pre-existing circumstances.

Do you have any strange or funny habits? Did you when you were a kid?

I walk with one foot almost perfectly in front of the other like someone on a runway. When I was a kid, I used to write almost exclusively in ballpoint pen because I didn't like pencil for anything but drawing.

What do you consider to be your greatest accomplishment?
Figuring out how to properly love and accept myself. Loving yourself has nothing to do with being completely pleased with all your features, but rather accepting that you are the only you that you will have, an understanding that you must be kind to yourself and that changing yourself for the better is also a form of love for yourself. Do I think I'm incredibly beautiful and perfect looking? Of course not. But my body is a home for my brain and my brain is doing its best, and I love them both fiercely for trying and for being mine. Do I think my personality is the best? No, but it is mine and I can and will learn to be better. Am I good at everything I try? Of course not! But I am good at some things and even if I am not the best in the world at those things, I still enjoy doing them. Life is so fragile and short. Being a person is very hard and very sad. Making sure to touch your weakest parts with soft hands is vital.

What would your readers be most surprised to learn about you?
I write sad things, but I'm very funny and fun in person. Most readers who I've met are always surprised about that.

THE UNIVERSE IS FULL OF SECOND CHANCES.

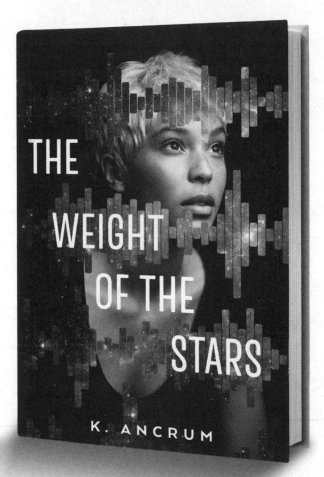

Keep reading for a sneak peek.

DAWN

She woke up to the sound of screaming.

She *always* woke up to the sound of screaming. Ryann scrunched her eyes against it for a minute, and then rubbed her face in exhaustion. Eventually, she heaved herself from bed and lumbered into the living room.

"Hey, *heyheyhey*," she whispered. "It's okay."

She picked up Charlie and put him in his rocker on the floor, tipping it gently back and forth with her foot as she opened the fridge.

Her younger brother, James, was still snoring loudly a couple rooms over, but she waited until Charlie was clean and fed to pop her head in and wake him up.

"Get up, it's six forty-five."

James just sighed and flopped over.

"Seriously, James." Ryann pushed herself into James's room, kicking dirty clothes and magazines out of the way. She yanked his dresser open and pulled out a pair of torn jeans and a black T-shirt and tossed them on James's bed.

"I'm leaving in ten minutes." She slammed the door shut behind her.

15 MINUTES

Ryann wiped Charlie's face clean and buttoned him up into his cold-weather onesie. She packed the baby some food, and then dropped him off with their neighbor Ms. Worthing.

By the time she got back, James was awake, dressed, and smoking on the front stairs.

"Did you eat yet?" she asked.

He stared at Ryann blankly, eyes bleary with exhaustion. His purple hair was a tangled nest. Ryann sighed in exasperation and went back inside so that she could grab some granola bars and her leather jacket.

She tossed one bar into his lap on her way out and hopped onto her motorcycle. Ryann waited patiently until she felt James sluggishly climb on behind her and put his arms loosely around her waist. Then she took off up the highway to the next town over.

The Bird siblings had had many good things snatched from them.

Their father had been a handyman with a small business and loyal clients. He'd had a big red beard and large hands and a laugh that echoed over fields and hills. Their mother had been a mathematician working for NASA. They loved their wild tall girl and small round boy as best they could. But, one bright morning, they died. Sometimes, people just die.

A little while afterward, James stopped talking altogether. Then, a year later he brought a baby home. A baby with red hair, owlish eyes, and a laugh that echoed. Ryann had questions, but James never answered them. And like on that terrible bright morning a year before, she swallowed hard, tightened her shoelaces, and stood up to meet it.

So there they were:

Sitting in the ruins of the best that they could build.

And it would always have to be enough.

45 MINUTES

There was a larger town near to the one Ryann Bird lived in. Ryann drove them miles to get there every morning.

It didn't have a trailer park where girls could live, snug with their little brother and his baby. Or a Laundromat where most of the machines were broken. Or a big parking lot that was supposed to become a grocery store, but didn't.

This town had a school and a mall and the sort of families that made sure both kids ate their breakfast before they left the house. Who drove them to school in luxury cars and made sure they had school supplies.

It was the best in the district. They were lucky it was that close.

Ryann tucked her bike behind the school in the lot where teachers liked to park. James hopped off, smacked her on the shoulder in thanks, and ran to class. Ryann swung her book-bag over her shoulder and walked slowly into the building.

Ryann was always late, so she didn't bother to hurry. She used to run to get to her seat, but none of the teachers ever gave her a break so she just figured, why even bother?

She knew what she looked like, and she looked like trouble. So, she was nearly always in it regardless of the circumstances.

Ryann had been trimming her wild black hair herself since junior year and it showed. After the bright morning accident, she had a deep scar on one cheekbone and no matter how much concealer she used, nothing ever quite hid it. Then, to make things worse, she'd become so exhausted and red-eyed since Charlie arrived that she kept getting accused of being high even though she didn't even smoke. She looked meaner and harder than she had any business looking at this nice rich school in this nice rich neighborhood. So, she just became what she looked like. It was easier than fighting it.

Ryann slammed the door open and walked in, passing right in front of the room, obscuring the light of the projector.

"Always a pleasure, Ryann," Mrs. Marsh, their history teacher, drawled sarcastically.

Ryann trudged to a chair in the back of the room. She dropped her bookbag on the floor, then tapped the kid in front of her on the back to ask for a pencil. Jefferson, who sat in front of her most of the time and generally had loads of pencils, waved his empty pencil case. He reached forward and tapped the girl in front of him on the shoulder.

"Hey. Ryann Bird needs a pencil."

The girl didn't even turn around. She just sat ramrod straight in her chair and said very quietly. "Ryann can bring her own pencils to school. Just like everyone else."

It was deafeningly quiet. Mrs. Marsh cleared her throat meaningfully.

"Any student who needs a pencil can get one from the pencil jar on the front of my desk." she said, looking at Ryann pointedly.

Ryann got up, went to the front of the room, and grabbed a few.

As she walked back to her desk, she reached out and let her fingertips glide over the top of the desk of the girl who'd denied her. As gentle and silent as a promise.